SHELTER

Random House  New York

SHELTER

CHRISTIE MATHESON

Text copyright © 2021 by Christie Matheson
Jacket art copyright © 2021 by Kathrin Honesta

All rights reserved. Published in the United States by
Random House Children's Books,
a division of Penguin Random House LLC, New York.

Random House and the colophon are registered trademarks
of Penguin Random House LLC.

Visit us on the Web! rhcbooks.com

Educators and librarians, for a variety of teaching tools,
visit us at RHTeachersLibrarians.com

Library of Congress Cataloging-in-Publication Data
Name: Matheson, Christie, author.
Title: Shelter / Christie Matheson.
Description: First edition. | New York : Random House, [2021] | Summary: While
ten-year-old Maya attends an elite private school on scholarship, her classmates
are unaware that she and her family are living in a homeless shelter, but on one
poignant day Maya discovers having a house is not the only way to have a home.
Identifiers: LCCN 2020044870 (print) | LCCN 2020044871 (ebook) |
ISBN 978-0-593-37638-6 (trade) | ISBN 978-0-593-37639-3 (lib. bdg.) |
ISBN 978-0-593-37641-6 (ebook)
Subjects: CYAC: Homeless persons—Fiction. | Shelters for the homeless—
Fiction. | Schools—Fiction. | Family life—Fiction.
Classification: LCC PZ7.M424764 Sh 2021 (print) |
LCC PZ7.M424764 (ebook) | DDC [Fic]—dc23

Printed in the United States of America
10 9 8 7 6 5 4 3 2 1
First Edition

For Ellie

SHELTER

It is in the shelter of each other
that the people live.

—IRISH PROVERB

6:32 a.m. I open my eyes. Through a small window, I see a hint of light in the winter morning sky. That tells me it's time to wake up.

But I curl my legs tighter to my chest under my blanket. I didn't sleep very well, partly because it was one of those nights when my feet never got all the way warm. Outside the blanket will be even chillier, and I'm not ready to leave the relative warmth of my little nest. I also have an ache in my stomach, and I can't feel if it's because I'm sad or because I'm anxious about everything that's happening today. Probably both. It's not easy to get out of bed when you have that waking-up ache.

Still, I know if I don't get up now, I'll be late to school. I don't want to be late. It's a Friday, and I have a ninety-minute art period today. Plus, as exhausting as school can be, at least being there feels almost normal. Unlike every other part of my life.

Slowly, I peel my blanket off, sit up, and glance out the window again. There's no sign of rain, but I heard my PE teacher say yesterday that it's going to *pour* today. As if today weren't going to be hard enough already.

I swing my feet onto the floor. Yikes. It's cold.

San Francisco, where I live, doesn't get freezing the way some places do. But on wet winter days, it's chilly. And this room, which never gets much sunlight and is heated by a system that only works some of the time, is especially cold.

I know that in many ways I'm lucky to live in San Francisco. It's supposed to rain later, but the temperature should reach fifty degrees today. There are parts of Iowa and Minnesota where it will be *negative* fifty with the windchill factor.

I shiver in my pajamas, which are getting thin and are too short for me. I've had them since I was eight. I'm almost eleven now. They have pink and red hearts on them, which is perfect for February, and today is February 1. But I wear them all year long. They've been my favorites for a long time, and right now they're the only pajamas I have. I take them off, shivering, and fold them so I can wear them again tonight.

As quietly as I can, I pull on navy blue leggings and a white shirt. The leggings have a hole in the left knee, and the shirt is stained in the front. No matter how hard I scrub it, that stain won't come out. But when I pull my blue-and-white-plaid school uniform jumper over them, the hole and stain are barely noticeable. And at least my leggings and shirt are all the way dry this morning. Knowing how chilly and rainy today's going to get, I do not want to start with a wet uniform. I wash my clothes every night, because if you wear anything that still smells like yesterday's PE class, there are kids at my school who will definitely make fun of you for it.

A few days ago my clothes were still damp from being washed the night before, but I had to wear them anyway.

Like my heart pajamas, they're the only ones I have.

I put on my white socks, which thankfully are also completely dry. They're worn through at the heels, but they feel better than the bare floor, at least. I lace up my white school sneakers, which aren't very white anymore.

The arms of my navy blue school sweatshirt are getting short, but I need something warmer than a short-sleeved shirt today, so I put it on. I brush my long hair and pull it into the tight braid Mama insists on, every single day. "We don't need to deal with lice right now," she reminds me if I ever try to skip the braid. She's not kidding. I did get lice once. About ten girls at my school had it. It's a pain to get rid of lice, and expensive to pay for treatment. Since then, my hair always goes into a braid for school.

I'm almost ready to make the journey across the city to my school, a private girls' school about four miles away. Today I'll have to ride two city buses to get there. I need to leave soon.

Mama and my little sister, Gabby, usually go with me on the ride to school, and when they do, we only take one bus. Except for yesterday. Mama and Gabby were with me, but we were practicing for today, when we knew I'd be making the trip to school alone. Because Mama has a job interview, finally, this morning. If she rides the bus to school with me, she might be late for it. And then she has to be at the hospital in the afternoon, so she can't pick me up from school, either.

So I have to go by myself. Both ways. And probably in the rain, at least on the way home. I know it's not fair for me to be mad at Mama about this. I'm trying not to be. But no one else at my school is going to have to do what I have to do today.

Mama doesn't want me walking to the farther-away bus stop without her. Instead, I'll go to the closer bus stop, but that means changing buses halfway through the trip. It also means the whole ride takes longer.

I check my backpack to make sure my homework folder is in there. Of course it is; I put it there last night and checked three times. Homework is due on Fridays, and I have never turned my homework in late. Not even after what happened to my dad. Not even with everything that's been going on with Mama, Gabby, and me.

Plus, if you turn your homework folder in during homeroom on Friday morning, you get it back by Friday afternoon so you can take it home over the weekend to work on the next week's homework. That gives me something to do over the weekend, and it usually feels good to read my teachers' comments on my work from the previous week.

With my backpack on, I lean over the cot where Mama is sleeping with Gabby. It's close to the mattress on the floor where I slept. So far I've managed not to wake them up, even though I've been getting dressed about three feet away from them.

Mama and Gabby usually wake up earlier than I do. My sister had a hard time falling asleep last night, though, and even after she fell asleep, she tossed and turned and cried out a lot. Then a loud noise from out-side woke her up, and she had trouble falling asleep all over again. Which means Mama and I didn't sleep very well, either, but we can handle it better than a two-and-a-half-year-old can.

So I know Gabby should probably sleep as long as possible this morning. But I need to wake up Mama now, to tell her I'm leaving for school, and to make sure she's up in time to get ready for her day. She can't be late to her interview.

Usually the first thing I do when I see Mama in the morning is kiss her. If I ever have to wake her up, I kiss her forehead. But I'm still kind of mad at her. So I just tap her cheek. Nothing. I tap it again. She groans in her sleep, and then her eyes flutter open. When she sees me, she smiles.

"Good morning, my Maya," she whispers. At the sound of her voice, some of my anger melts away.

"Good morning, my Mama," I whisper back.

Then I kiss my little sister on the forehead and whisper, ever so quietly, "Good morning to you, Gabby girl."

I leave it to Mama to wake her up, because Gabby is sure to be grumpy after such a tough night. "I'm leaving for school now, Mama," I whisper.

When I say that, Mama's eyes open wide and she sits up. She puts her hand on my cheek.

"Oh, my Maya," she whispers, and I think I see tears in her eyes.

I know she wishes she could take me to school today, like she does every other day. I think she *really* wishes she could just walk me to school, like she used to. "Look at you, all ready to go. I'm sorry I didn't wake up first."

"It's okay," I whisper. "Last night was hard."

We both glance at Gabby, who is now finally sleeping deeply. Mama reaches over and strokes Gabby's head softly. Then she looks back at me.

"Do you remember exactly how to do the buses today?" Mama asks.

"I do. I remember. It's fine, Mama," I say, the ache swelling in my stomach and some of my anger coming back. I try to sound confident, even though I'm nervous. But people, even kids my age, take the bus by themselves all the time. It will be fine. It just doesn't feel fine right now.

"Did you take a banana?" she asks.

"I will," I say, glancing at the two remaining bananas on the shelf near the door. I decide I actually won't take one, so Mama and Gabby will have something to eat.

"You are amazing, my love. I'm so sorry I can't take you today. I'll see you here after you take the bus back from school. Have a beautiful day, my Maya." I can feel more of my anger melting away.

"I will, my Mama. You too. Good luck," I whisper. "And tell Daddy I love him."

"I will," she whispers back. "Thank you."

I pause near the bananas, to make her think I'm grabbing one, and I notice there are three left, not two. I leave them all. My school lunch will come soon enough, and Gabby gets hungry in the morning. She can have two bananas if she wants.

I'm not really mad at Mama. I'm definitely not mad at Gabby. I'm just sad and scared.

So I turn and blow a kiss toward them. Then I quietly open the door of our room, close and lock it behind me, and walk down the hall of our homeless shelter.

1

Go TiMe

Start where you are.

—ARTHUR ASHE

6:56 a.m. There's a clock near the front door of the shelter, and I realize it's not quite seven a.m. Mama doesn't like us to leave the shelter before seven. She thinks there are more people around outside after seven. She's probably right, although I'm not sure four minutes makes a big difference.

While I wait, and brace myself for the trip to school that I've been dreading, I look around. We've been living here for exactly one month. Although it feels like much longer than that. When every day is long and hard, time feels different. A month can feel like forever.

Anyway, it *is* a homeless shelter, but no one who works here calls it that. They call it a family shelter,

9

which I guess they think sounds nicer. There are lots of different kinds of shelters, I've learned. Some are just for grown-ups, some are for men only, some are for women only, some are for kids who've run away from home, and some are only for families with kids. Some are transitional housing shelters, where you can stay for more than a year. Some shelters have private rooms, and some have a bunch of beds in one big room. Some let you stay for a while and leave your stuff there, and some you can use only at night—you have to leave during the day and you might or might not get a bed the next night.

We had to stay at one of those one-night-at-a-time shelters, for one night, before we moved in here.

But even if you add up all the beds and all the rooms, there aren't enough shelters for the thousands of home-less people in San Francisco. There are waiting lists, and there are a lot of people who sleep in their cars or outside.

Here we have our own room and even our own bath-room with a sink and a toilet. And there's a shared bath-room where we can take showers sometimes. We can stay for up to six months. I know we're lucky to have our own space. But I don't want to be here for that long. I also don't know where we'll go next, if Mama doesn't have a job by then.

I didn't think much about shelters before we had to move into one. I mean, I knew a little about them. Every year at school we talk about homelessness, hunger, and food insecurity—that's when someone doesn't always have enough food—in San Francisco. Our class also goes to work at a local food pantry one afternoon during each school year, to help with food distribution. That food pantry is at a community center in a neighborhood called the Richmond.

The Richmond isn't one of the San Francisco neighborhoods you see on postcards. It's far away from the steep cable car hills, crooked Lombard Street, and the sea lions at Pier 39.

The Richmond is bordered by some fancy neighborhoods, Golden Gate Park, and the Presidio, which is a national park with hiking trails. But basically it's just a normal neighborhood.

Some streets have nice houses, and some blocks have run-down apartment buildings. It's safe, for a city neighborhood.

It's where my family used to live.

When we volunteered at the shelter, we learned that 25 percent of people who live in the Richmond are at high risk for food insecurity.

And now my family is, too.

7:02 a.m. Just in case the clock is fast, I wait until the minute hand is a couple of notches past the twelve. Mama was right—there actually are more people walking around now than there were a few minutes ago. When she's with me, I don't pay as much attention to things like that. I take a deep breath and remember that if anything scary happens, I can run right back to the front door of the shelter.

Our shelter is on the edge of a neighborhood called the Tenderloin. Unlike the Richmond, a lot of the Tenderloin isn't safe, even by city standards. If you were to look up a crime map of San Francisco, which I did once at school, you would see that a lot of bad stuff happens around here.

Crimes happen more often at night and very early in the morning, while it's still dark, and when there aren't as many people around. But that doesn't mean nothing bad can happen during the day. I try to tell myself that nothing will happen today, though, and remind myself that I can run fast if I need to. I was one of the fastest fifth graders on my school's cross-country team last fall. That feels like a long time ago.

I push the door open and step outside.

As the cold, damp air hits me, I shiver. I wish I had one of those really warm puffy jackets that most of the girls at my school have. Or a warm raincoat, today. Or that the sleeves of my sweatshirt were longer.

At least it's not raining. Yet.

I look around quickly to make sure nothing scary is happening on the sidewalk.

The people who sleep here at night have mostly cleaned up their tents and boxes, but there's a man lying right up against the next building, in a dirty orange sleeping bag. I'm going to have to walk past him.

Sometimes homeless people scare me. That might not make sense, because we're homeless now, and I'm not scared of us. I'm not scared of the families we've met at our shelter, either. And I know it's not fair for me to say I'm scared of a whole group of people. I'm not.

But there was one time when a homeless woman followed us for half a block, screaming at Mama about giving her some money.

Another time, a homeless man came out of his tent when we were walking by and asked us if he could sing to us. That wasn't as scary as the screaming, but it startled me when he jumped out at us.

And then one time a man pulled down his pants in front of us and started peeing on a fire hydrant. That sounds like it might have been funny, but it wasn't. Anyway, I just never know exactly what's going to happen. And when I'm by myself, that's scary.

I grip my backpack straps a little tighter and walk quickly down the block, knowing I can break into a run if I need to. I'm a fast runner. It will be okay.

And then, just as I'm approaching the man in the sleeping bag, someone screams. As the sound rips through the air, I don't think. I run.

* * *

7:04 a.m. I'm about ten feet past the man in the sleeping bag when I realize that the scream didn't come from him, or from anyone on my sidewalk. Across the street, a woman is screaming down to a man from an open window two stories up. And the man is shouting back at her, using a bunch of words Mama has told me *never* to say. They have no idea I can hear their yelling, or that the first piercing scream made my whole body go cold with fear.

I try to catch my breath, and I glance back at the man in the sleeping bag. He hasn't budged. He's curled up into a tight ball, and his eyes are clenched shut. I realize he's probably freezing, and that he probably just wants to get some sleep.

I feel my breathing slowing down. Now I feel guilty for being scared of him. And sorry that he couldn't find a bed inside last night.

7:06 a.m. At the end of the block I wait for the walk signal, jogging in place to stay warm and keeping watch all around me. When the light changes, I make sure no cars are about to speed through the red light, and that drivers are actually paying attention and aren't going to turn into my crosswalk. I know what can happen if someone is texting while driving. Then I cross to the bus stop to wait for the number 2 bus. I'm glad that a few other people are waiting as well.

I notice they all have umbrellas. I don't have one. I look at the sky. It's full of dark gray clouds.

I wait for maybe three minutes, and then a bus pulls up. I swipe my bus pass through the card reader, and the driver gives me a smile. "Good morning, hon," she says. I smile back. "Good morning," I say. Most of the seats are filled, but there are two empty seats next to each other, pretty close to the front of the bus. I slide over to the window seat, clutch my backpack tightly as it rests on my lap, and stare outside. I can see a few traces of pink among the gray clouds in the sky, above the buildings.

The doors close and the bus heaves away. I unzip my backpack just a little and reach inside, feeling for my homework folder again. It's there, like I knew it would be. But it makes me feel better to check.

I reach in farther and feel for my worn-out copy of *Charlie and the Chocolate Factory*, one of my favorite books, and Gilbert, the little stuffed dog I've had since I was a baby.

When we left our house, we couldn't take much with us. We had to be able to carry it all. So I fit what I could into this backpack and one other bag. We can leave our stuff in our room at the shelter, but I always like to have my favorite things with me. Just in case.

Whenever I'm nervous or sad, I rub Gilbert's ear. There isn't much fur left on it, but it's still soft and comforting. I do that now. And it makes me feel less alone. I keep Gilbert in the zippered pocket at the back of the main compartment, for extra safekeeping—and so no one at school will see him.

The bus stops, the way it will many times on the way to my school. A crowd of people gets on, and I know I won't have an empty seat next to me for long. I hope if anyone sits next to me, it's someone nice.

A man gets on, practically shoving people out of his way, and complains loudly to the driver about the bus being late. Luckily, he pushes through the crowd, right past the seat next to me. An older woman, walking with a cane, spots it instead. I smile at her and she smiles at me.

I wonder what her story is. My dad used to say that everyone has a story. And especially since we've started meeting families at the shelter and learning how they got there, I know it's true. Everyone has a story. Most are complicated, and many are painful.

The woman sits down next to me, leans her head back against the seat, and closes her eyes. Whatever her story is, she must be tired.

I know how she feels.

*   *   *

7:15 a.m. The bus continues along Sutter Street. As we go, we pass fewer big buildings and more Victorian-style houses. There are a lot of Victorian houses in San Francisco. We learned about them in second grade, when we were studying the neighborhoods and architecture of the city. The Victorian houses in San Francisco have a lot of fancy woodwork and towers and other decorations on the outside.

Then we pass Japantown. We went there on a field trip in third grade. Japantown is smaller than Chinatown, but it's packed with Japanese shops and restaurants and tea and art, and it hosts beautiful festivals every year. It's also a place where some homeless people sleep.

Next we pass Fillmore Street, which has expensive shops and trendy (but, my dad always said, not the best) restaurants. Homeless people sleep around here, too. And then things get not-fancy again as we drive past a group of buildings that Mama told me is an affordable-housing development.

We haven't passed our old house yet. We won't do that until after I change buses. I know how to change buses, and I know where to do it, but it still feels strange to be doing it all alone.

7:22 a.m. The bus turns right onto Presidio Avenue and stops a few blocks later at the corner of California

Street, in front of the huge Jewish Community Center. This is where I get off to wait for my next bus. When I step down off the bus, the wind whips through me and I realize how warm the bus was. I hope the next one comes quickly.

I try to pull my sweatshirt sleeves down over my hands, but they're so short that I can only cover one hand at a time. The pink is all gone from the sky now, and the gray clouds have taken over. I really wish I had a coat.

I look east down California Street, straining to see if the next bus is in sight. It's not. I shiver and hunch my shoulders up near my ears. And wait.

7:28 a.m. Now I'm starting to worry. There are other people at the bus stop, and I know it's the right bus stop. But there's no bus here.

I'm freezing, and it's hard to think clearly when you're freezing.

A million things rush through my head. *The bus will never come. I'm going to be late to school. Maybe I should start walking. If I'm late, they'll call Mama. What if she tells them why I'm late? What if she tells them where I'm coming from? I don't want anyone to know where we're living.*

Just as my mind is about to spin out of control, I look

down California Street one more time and see it. The bus is coming. I'm shivering so hard now that my body is visibly shaking and my teeth are chattering. I can see one of the women at the bus stop looking at me with a mixture of sympathy and concern.

I grit my teeth and force myself to stop shaking so she'll assume I'm fine. *It's all good. Nothing to see here.* Maybe she'll think I just forgot my jacket, not that I don't have one.

The bus eases to a stop and the driver opens the doors. I let the worried lady get on first, so I can choose a seat far away from hers.

It's such a relief to get into the warmth. I grab my Clipper Card from my pocket and run it through the machine. Because we're now officially low-income and I'm a kid, I get to ride for free. Which is good, because we don't have money for bus passes and right now the bus is the only thing keeping me warm. I don't have to change buses again—this one takes me really close to my school.

I'm going to get off the bus a few stops early, though. There's a bus stop right near our old house, and I like to get off there. The house is on California Street, just a few blocks away from my school. It's not one of the big, fancy San Francisco houses, although there are plenty of those a few blocks away from it. In fact, our old house is one of the smallest houses in San Francisco.

It's part of a row of little cottages built in 1907, soon after the huge San Francisco earthquake of 1906. There were lots of cottages like ours built around then, because about 225,000 people were homeless after the earthquake. Most of the cottages have been torn down and replaced by apartment buildings.

My parents used to say they rented our cottage at just the right time, when prices had come down from crazy-high levels and before they went back up again to even crazier-high levels. And they joked about how small our house was compared to some of the enormous houses in this city. It doesn't seem very funny now.

We were always doing projects to take care of our house and fix it up. It was tiny, but it was pretty and cozy and comfortable. And I used to walk to school from it, every day.

If I get off this bus a few stops early, I can pretend for a few minutes that nothing has changed. That I'm just walking to school from home, like I always used to do.

7:33 a.m. I've stopped shivering, but I'm still thinking about our old house. I do this a lot lately. I loved it, but I never really thought about the fact that I was lucky to live there. When you have a house, it's easy to think you'll always have a house. And even if you like it, you don't necessarily think about how much you appreciate it.

Sometimes I even wished we had a bigger or fancier house, especially after I went to play dates or birthday parties in places where our little house would have fit into one room. Seriously.

I don't wish for a bigger or fancier house anymore.

All I want is our house.

Our little house, and my cozy room with a tiny window seat that was the perfect place to read. I could go into that little nook whenever I wanted and lose myself in the world of Ramona Quimby or Auggie Pullman or Ghost, Patina, Sunny, and Lu, or India Opal Buloni or Anne Shirley or Charlie Bucket.

When I was in the middle of reading *Charlie and the Chocolate Factory* (which I have read more times than I can count), I used to take out my piggy bank and count the money in it and imagine that I could give some of it to Charlie's family. Just a little extra money would have helped them so much.

I don't have my piggy bank anymore. It was too big to carry with me when we left our house. So I put the money from it ($17.32) into a plastic bag. That's in my backpack, too. I hug it a little tighter as the bus rumbles along.

*   *   *

7:40 a.m. The bus is getting closer to our old house now. This neighborhood feels like home. We pass Miss Lilly's Ballet, the studio where I used to take dance lessons, back when we could just barely afford something like that. I loved ballet—the classical music, the quiet focus on getting feet and arms in just the right positions. I also loved that my ballet teacher, Miss Lilly, had the same name as the ballet teacher in the Angelina Ballerina books.

Then the bus stops across the street from the coffee shop where my dad and I used to get hot chocolate on Saturday mornings.

Gabby is allergic to milk, and chocolate, and about a hundred other things. So it was something I did just with my dad.

I called it the hot chocolate store, because that's the only thing I ever got there. The owner always gave me extra whipped cream.

I miss hot chocolate.

And I really miss my dad.

2

MeMoRY TiMe

I am not what happened to me.

—CARL JUNG

7:42 a.m. For some reason, we aren't pulling away from the bus stop. And the bus driver is getting off. It's an electric bus, with trolley poles that connect to wires overhead for power. Sometimes the poles come off the wires and the driver has to fix them.

The bus is just sitting across from the hot chocolate store, and impatient drivers are honking because we're blocking the lane. I'm thinking about my dad, and our life before everything fell apart, and about how he'll respond to the procedure he had this week. Sometimes it feels like all we are—all I am—is homeless. And that all my dad is, is only a patient in a hospital. But that's not all we are.

That's just what has happened to us.

My dad is a writer. Was a writer. I don't know if I should say "was" or "is."

Anyway, he writes—wrote—about food and the environment. He talked a lot to us about food and its impact on the earth, especially if I ever asked for junk food. Except hot chocolate. I think that was because the hot chocolate store used organic milk and organic, fair-trade chocolate. He always thanked them for that.

He was a freelance writer, which meant he didn't have a job in just one place but wrote for a lot of different newspapers (including the biggest one in San Francisco) and magazines. He loved his work, and he was good at it, but I don't think he got paid much, at least compared to a lot of people around here.

Mama didn't get paid very much, either. She is a really good artist, and she used to be an art teacher.

When you combine two jobs that don't pay a lot, it doesn't add up to tons of money. And we live in one of the most expensive cities in the country. We've always had to watch every penny.

Luckily, because of rules in San Francisco, our land-lord couldn't raise our rent more than a little bit each year. He didn't mind. He liked our family. He had grandchildren, but they lived far away, and he said it made him happy to know we were living in his house.

Also, we didn't have to pay for my school, even

though it's a private school. Mama was the art teacher there for a long time, up until I was in second grade. So I got to go to school for free, and still do now, which is what my school does for all kids of teachers who worked there for a certain number of years. That's lucky. I love my school. Even if I don't love everyone who goes there.

7:47 a.m. The driver comes back onto the bus after fixing the trolley poles. "Sorry for the delay, folks," he says. And we start moving again, slowly at first, probably to make sure the poles stay on the wires.

We're approaching my old block. It's different from any other block on this part of California Street, because it has the row of little cottages in the middle instead of being packed with three- or four-story houses or apartment buildings. I love how the cottages all look together, even though some of them are run-down.

Well, one of them is pretty fancy now. That's part of our problem.

The cottage next door was sold right after Gabby was born. It had a sagging porch and peeling paint and broken windows and a leaky roof. The person who bought it basically ripped everything out and made it new on the inside and cleaned up the outside.

We didn't think much about it. But then a FOR SALE sign went up outside the fixed-up cottage. Mama looked up the price. It was a crazy amount of money. For a cottage the same size as ours.

Within a week, someone bought it. For even *more* money than the person selling the house was asking for.

I heard my parents talking about it one night. They were worried. They were pretty sure it wouldn't be long before our landlord told us he would be selling our house so he could make that kind of money.

They were right.

But that wasn't the only disaster we had coming.

7:52 a.m. We slow down and then stop across the street from my old house. It's under construction now, so the new owner can sell it for a lot of money, too. There's already a construction crew there this morning, working inside and out. The front door is open, and I can see into where our little living room used to be.

That's where we were when the phone call came last fall. It was a Friday afternoon in late October, and Mama was playing with Gabby on the rug while I sketched jack-o'-lantern faces. I was supposed to carve pumpkins with my dad the next day. He usually made pizza on Friday nights (gluten-free, egg-free, soy-free, nut-free, and dairy-free so Gabby could eat it, but still somehow really delicious).

But that day he wouldn't be home in time, because

he had a work meeting downtown. And we didn't have a car. We've never had one.

Sometimes my dad took the bus, but if the weather was good, he rode his bike. He used it to run errands and to get around the city for his work. He always wore his helmet. Including that Friday afternoon.

Hopefully the fact that he was wearing a helmet will end up saving his life. But we don't know yet.

Because on that Friday afternoon he was hit by a car. Witnesses said that the driver of the car was looking at his phone and that he ran a red light and sped through an intersection. There's a reason you're not supposed to text and drive. You could kill someone. Or almost kill someone.

My dad had what the doctors called a traumatic brain injury. If he hadn't been wearing a helmet, they said, he would have died. He also had severe pulmonary contusions, which means his lungs were badly bruised. They had to put in a breathing tube so a ventilator could help him breathe. The doctors have been keeping him sedated (which is kind of like sleeping) while he's on the ventilator. So they can't really tell how his brain is doing.

This week he had a procedure called a tracheostomy, so the ventilator now attaches to a breathing tube that goes in through his neck instead of his mouth. I don't understand it all, but now that they've done that, they can slowly take him off the sedatives and let him wake up—and find out if he can breathe on his own. That's why Mama is going to the hospital today, after her interview. To see him when he might be awake, and when the doctors check to see if he can breathe on his own.

No one is sure yet if he'll be able to.

Or if his brain will work anymore.

7:53 a.m. When the bus driver opens the doors, I hop off so I can walk the rest of the way to school. I take one more look at our cottage, then hitch my backpack up on my shoulders and start walking. It's about five blocks from here to the front gate of my school, and there are always people out walking dogs, and cars going by— many with girls from my school inside. Sometimes people I know see me and ask if I want a ride, but I never do. And that's not just because of where I live now. I like walking places and being outside and thinking.

Today as I walk, I keep thinking about my dad. When she was pregnant with Gabby, Mama made a plan that after the baby was born, she would take one school year off from work to be with her, and then go back to teaching at my school. But Gabby had trouble gaining weight and kept getting rashes and throwing up. It took a while to figure out what was going on, but her pediatrician realized she had a bunch of food allergies.

Mama was breastfeeding Gabby, so she stopped eating anything with dairy, soy, gluten, eggs, fish, or nuts, and Gabby started to get better.

Mama got nervous about going back to work. She wanted to be with Gabby to feed her and help her grow and to "get her back on track developmentally." Because when a baby doesn't gain enough weight and gets sick a lot, she can be slow to do other things (like sit up and crawl and walk).

And then my dad got a dream writing job. He was going to help a famous chef write a cookbook, and a publishing company was going to pay him a lot of money to do it. It was enough that he could pay for health insurance and Mama could stay home with Gabby for a few years.

It was perfect.

For a while.

7:54 a.m. When the car sped into my dad, his work bag was crushed. His laptop computer was inside his work bag. The laptop was destroyed. And the laptop had the cookbook manuscript stored on it.

Mama is sure he must have backed it up somewhere, somehow. But she hasn't been able to find it. And that doesn't matter. He won't get paid more money until the whole manuscript is turned in. Which means we didn't get any of the money we were expecting to live on this year.

Then, less than a week after my dad's accident, we got a letter from our landlord letting us know he was selling our house. He felt terrible about the timing, he said, but he'd received an offer from a developer that was too good to turn down. He did say if we could match the offer, he'd be happy to sell the house to us instead. But of course we couldn't do that. So we had until the end of the year to get out.

And because we *had* to keep paying for my dad's private health insurance, we were going to run out of rent money before then.

Of course we didn't have enough money to rent a new place.

And that's how we became homeless.

3

SCHooL TiMe

You must do the thing you think you cannot do.

—ELEANOR ROOSEVELT

7:55 a.m. I walk past the entrance gate of a neighborhood called Sea Cliff, which is full of fancy houses. Abby, my best friend, just moved there last month. The same day we moved into the shelter, actually.

I went to her old house about a million times. Abby and I have been best friends since the first day of kindergarten.

I've always been shy and quiet, and I've always been happiest when I'm making art, so during our first free-choice period that day, I was in the corner, drawing, alone.

Abby came right up to me and said hi. "You look nice. I can tell," she said. "And I like your drawing."

31

I wasn't sure how to respond. She looked nice to me, too. But I didn't say anything.

"Can I draw with you?" she asked.

I nodded. She stayed. From that day on, we've been a team.

7:56 a.m. I look into Sea Cliff and can see just the tippy-top of Abby's house down the street. When her family first bought the house, before my dad's accident, we were so excited that we would be living near each other. She could see the top of our cottage from the window of the room that would become her bedroom. Our parents said we'd even be able to walk to each other's houses by ourselves.

Walking by yourself to your best friend's house might not sound like a big deal, but when you're ten years old and you live in a city, it is. And we were really excited about it. We had to wait, though, because the house was being renovated before they moved in. And by the time they moved in, we had moved out.

I can't walk to Abby's house from our shelter.

Abby doesn't know where we're living. She knows we moved out of our cottage, but I didn't tell her where we were going. Which I know she thinks is weird, because I've told her everything for as long as we've been friends. If I were going to tell anyone, I would tell her. I haven't yet, though. It's a hard thing to say to someone.

Abby's new house is much, much, much bigger than my old house. So was her old house. But not in the feels-like-a-hotel kind of way. They had a beautiful kitchen and lots of art and pretty windows. But it always felt cozy and homey. I loved going to her house. I'll bet I'd love her new house, too.

They moved to their new house because it has an elevator. Not because they just want an elevator, but because having an elevator will make things much easier for Abby's parents and her younger sister.

Abby's sister was born with cerebral palsy. She can't walk without help or climb stairs. She also can't hear, and she can't really speak, either, although she and her family have come up with ways to communicate.

When she was little, her parents could carry her when they needed to, but now she's almost seven. The elevator will help them a lot.

Knowing Abby has taught me that even people with really nice houses have hard things going on.

Earlier this year, my humanities teacher, Ms. Choi, shared a good quote with us: "Be kind, for everyone you meet is fighting a hard battle." She said a lot of people think Plato said that, but it more likely came from something a Scottish minister said. Whoever said it, I like it.

It reminds me of my dad saying everyone has a story. Because it's true. There's always something going on, sometimes something very sad or painful or difficult, behind what you see on the surface.

There certainly is for me.

I'm getting closer to school now. I'm relieved that I made it all on my own, and I'm a little worn out from the journey. Just getting here today was a battle for me.

But being here doesn't mean my battle is over. And I'm not sure everyone will be kind.

7:58 a.m. I approach my school's entrance gate and see a long parade of cars waiting in the drop-off line. As much as I like the walk from my old house to school, this is the part of my walk where, every school day, I have to force myself to keep going. Because I get scared. Scared that one mean comment will make me cry so hard that I can't stop. Scared someone will guess I'm homeless. Scared because no one here knows my secret—Mama thought we should tell my teachers, but I begged her not to. Scared because I just don't know what's coming.

When I told Mama how scared I get before school, she asked me to be brave. I told her I'm not brave. I'm scared. And then she said that being brave doesn't mean not being scared. It means being scared and doing something anyway. And that we all have to do hard things.

As I get close to the gate, I try to be brave.

I hear someone call my name.

I look toward the car line and see Abby's dad's car. Abby and her little sister, Serena, are in the backseat, and they're both waving to me. It's hard for Serena to control her muscles enough for a wave to look like what you might expect a wave to look like, but I know what she's doing—and I think she's smiling, too. I walk closer to the car. "Hi, Abby," I say. Serena wouldn't hear me if I said hi, but I wave at her with a big smile. "Hi, Mr. Prescott," I add.

"Hi, Maya!" Mr. Prescott says. "We've missed you, kiddo. How's your mom doing?"

Abby's family knows about my dad, of course. They helped us a lot after the accident, letting Gabby and me stay with them while Mama was at the hospital with my dad.

It's hard for Mama to leave Gabby anywhere, but the Prescotts are really careful about Gabby's allergies and she's always been okay with them. Abby and I were already friends when Gabby was born. Gabby's real name is Gabriela, but Abby loves that Gabby's nickname rhymes with her name. I love that, too.

Before the accident, Abby and I used to spend tons of time at each other's houses. We had a sleepover at one of our houses almost every other weekend.

When Mama and I realized we were going to lose

our house, and that we didn't have anywhere else to go, I asked Mama why we couldn't just stay with the Prescotts. "They're moving into a new house," I said. "And it's even bigger than the one they have now!"

"Oh, sweetie," Mama said. "They've been so good to us, but that's just too much to ask of anyone. And they have enough to deal with."

I knew she was probably right. But that didn't keep me from wishing we could stay there. Or that we had some family living nearby. Or someplace, anyplace, to go.

A few days later, we learned that a room was opening at our shelter. We were very lucky, Mama said. Some families have to wait months—or more—for space in a shelter. On the first day of the new year, we moved in.

Abby and I haven't had a single sleepover since.

8:00 a.m. The Prescotts' car is almost at the front of the car line. I walk slowly alongside them and wait for Abby to get out so we can walk into school together. When Mr. Prescott stops the car, Abby unbuckles her seat belt, gives Serena a kiss, and hops out of the car. "Bye, Dad," she calls.

"Have a great day, kiddos," Mr. Prescott says to us. "Love you, Ab! Come see us, Maya!"

Abby and I walk side by side toward the main gate,

not saying anything, although it seems like she keeps starting a sentence and then stopping before anything gets out.

The head of our school, Ms. Thompson, is at the gate, waiting to say good morning to every girl. She gives us fist bumps as we walk in and says, "Happy Friday, Abby and Maya!"

"Good morning, Ms. Thompson," we say in unison. Then we continue up the walkway that leads from the entrance gate into school. We're quiet until we get close to the entrance, when Abby finally says something. "Do you think . . . can we have a sleepover this weekend?" She sounds a little nervous when she says it.

It feels like there's a knot in my stomach. I don't want my best friend to feel nervous asking about a sleepover. Or sad because I keep saying no. She can tell something is off with me, not just because my dad is in the hospital. And she has no idea why.

I've had weirdness with a friend before, and it feels awful. But Abby and I have never had any drama. Until now. Although I'm not sure "drama" is the right word for this.

Last year, when I was in fourth grade, one of my other friends, Lucy, suddenly stopped wanting to hang out with me. I'd known her since preschool, and just like that she started ignoring me.

She'd begun spending all her time with a girl in our

class named Sloane, and if I ever tried to play with them at recess, they'd whisper as I approached and make me feel uncomfortable the whole time. Pretty soon, it became pretty obvious that Lucy was ditching me, and I stopped trying. But it still hurts my feelings that she'd rather be friends with Sloane than with me.

Once upon a time, back in kindergarten, I thought Sloane and I might become friends. Near the beginning of the year, her mother emailed Mama to see if I could come for a play date. First she picked us both up from school in a car that was practically as big our cottage—and then I saw their house. "House" isn't the right word. It's a mansion.

When we climbed the stairs from the enormous garage, which had five cars in it, we ended up in an even bigger foyer. And I was confused. It was huge. I mean *huge*. There were tall flower arrangements everywhere and a shiny marble floor (I remember noticing the sound of Sloane's mom's high heels clicking on it) and a massive staircase and a gigantic chandelier. And on one side there was an elevator.

"Do you live in a hotel?" I asked eagerly, thinking about *Eloise at the Plaza.*

Sloane snickered. Her mother gave me a sort of pitying smile and shook her head, saying, "No, dear. This is our *home.*"

I still didn't understand. "All of it?" I asked.

"Yes, dear," her mother said, glancing at her sparkly watch as we waited for Sloane's nanny to come down the stairs and take us into the gleaming kitchen for a snack. Once she'd given some quick instructions to the nanny, we didn't see Sloane's mom again.

After our snack, Sloane's nanny took us to the playroom, which was big enough for an indoor bouncy house and indoor trampoline. It had a door out to the backyard, where an outdoor bouncy house and outdoor trampoline awaited, along with a swing set, tree house, and twisty slide. The yard was enormous, twice the size of the biggest backyard I'd ever seen in San Francisco. It backed right up to another huge house.

"Can we play out there?" I asked excitedly.

"I guess so," Sloane said, with zero enthusiasm.

"Do your neighbors come play in your yard, too?" I asked once we were outside.

"What neighbors?" she asked.

I pointed to the big house that shared her backyard.

"Oh, that. That's our house," Sloane explained.

"But . . ." I looked back at the house we'd just come from. "*That's* your house."

She rolled her eyes, something I'd seen her mom do while talking to the nanny. "They're *both* our houses. We wanted a big yard, and of course we didn't want to share. So we bought that house, too."

I stared at her.

"So you have two houses? Right next to each other?" I asked.

"Yes," she said impatiently.

"Do you live in both of them?" I asked.

"Not really. Sometimes guests stay there. Can you stop asking me questions now?"

"Okay," I said.

We bounced on the trampoline for about three minutes before Sloane got bored.

"Let's go play *Nail Salon* on iPads," she said.

Which we did. But I didn't think it was very much fun. I kept looking outside to the trampoline and the huge backyard.

Then Sloane got frustrated with the game, stamped her foot, and *threw* her iPad across the room. It hit the wall with a loud smack. I stared in disbelief. I couldn't believe she'd done that.

When her nanny came running to see what the loud noise was, Sloane announced, without hesitation, "*She* did it," and pointed at me. I opened my mouth in shock. I couldn't believe she'd lied like that. I'm not sure whether the nanny believed her, given that I was sitting calmly, holding the iPad I'd been using. But she did tell me that in Sloane's house, throwing things was not okay.

"But I didn't—" I started to protest, until Sloane shot me one of the most frightening looks I've ever seen. *Shut. Up,* she mouthed.

No one had ever talked to me like that. I didn't know what to do or say. Apparently a thrown iPad wasn't a big deal in that house, because Sloane's nanny didn't say another word about it. I got the feeling it wasn't the first time Sloane had thrown something.

At that point, all I wanted was for Mama to come and pick me up. It's almost like she knew, because she rang the doorbell about two minutes later. We met her in that huge foyer with the marble floor and the enormous chandelier. I saw her glance around for a second, taking it all in, but she didn't say anything about it. She just scooped me up and gave me a huge hug and said, "Hi, my Maya."

She put me down, and I turned to say goodbye to Sloane, who was, to my surprise, staring at us and looking sad. But then she snapped her stare into a glare, spun around, and disappeared to somewhere else in the house without saying goodbye. Mama and I said goodbye to Sloane's nanny, and thanked her for having me, and then got out of there.

I never did get invited back.

And Sloane hasn't been nice to me since.

8:02 a.m. I hope Abby doesn't think I'm ditching her like Lucy ditched me.

"I would love to have a sleepover. I really, really,

really would love to. But . . ." I swallow hard and think about telling her everything. I wonder what she'd say. I look around. I can't do it now. There are too many people here. And we don't have enough time.

"Are you worried about leaving your mom? Because I can come to your house!" she said. "We can take care of Gabby and give your mom a little break," she says.

That's the kind of friend Abby is. No one else I know would even think of something like that, trying to help a tired parent. Oh, how I wish she could come to our house for a sleepover. I imagine eating pizza together, playing charades, and staying up too late whispering in my old room.

And I start to cry.

8:03 a.m. Abby looks worried. "Hey," she says kindly. "What's going on?"

Then she realizes what she's said and adds, quietly, "I mean, other than everything with your dad."

For the first time, I'm about to tell her the truth. And maybe say yes to a sleepover. At her house, obviously. It just sounds so nice. We would eat a yummy dinner, get into pajamas (she could let me borrow ones that actually fit), and get under blankets on her big, comfortable couch to watch a movie. And I could sleep in a real bed.

At her old house she had two beds in her room, and I'm pretty sure she does at her new house, too.

Then again, I don't want to leave Mama and Gabby alone in the shelter, even for one night. That doesn't seem fair somehow. I think it helps when we're all together.

I open my mouth to speak, and then I see Sloane, Lucy, and their friend Madison approaching. They're staring at Sloane's phone, laughing about something. They all have long, shiny hair that hangs down as they lean their heads together. Without thinking, I reach up and touch my mandatory braid. Obviously their parents aren't worried about paying for lice treatment.

The three of them are wearing shiny black rain-coats and high, shiny rain boots. I'm pretty sure those boots cost more than a hundred dollars, and you only need them about eight times per year in San Francisco. I think Sloane has at least three different pairs. Today she's wearing dark purple ones. She also has them in navy blue and black, and from a distance they're pretty much impossible to tell apart. Looking closely, I see that Madison and Lucy are wearing purple ones today, too.

I've never had rain boots like that. Even before the accident and the shelter, my family couldn't afford them. I've always been the kid in used uniforms and hand-me-down school sneakers. Which used to make me a little self-conscious, but the truth is that almost no one notices. Most people pay more attention to what they're wearing than what you're wearing. But still, sometimes I wished I could have the same stuff everyone else had— the rain boots, sure, but also the brand-name bags and expensive sneakers. Oh, and the diamond earrings. I don't even have my ears pierced. I used to beg to get my ears pierced. Not because I even wanted diamonds. It just felt like all the other girls had pierced ears, and I wanted them, too.

Since my dad's accident, though, I care a whole lot less about all that. Boots don't matter. Earrings don't matter.

Families matter.

I try to shift my face into not-crying mode and hope they'll keep staring at the phone as they walk past us. But nope. I'm not that lucky. They look up. Sloane peers at me. "Are you *crying?*" she asks, in her trying-to-sound-like-a-teenager voice. I know she isn't expecting an answer. As they keep walking, she whispers something and Madison laughs. Lucy doesn't. She just looks uncomfortable. And she doesn't quite look at me.

Abby shakes her head and rolls her eyes, then looks back at me. She waits for me to say what I was about to say. But I don't. I can't right now. A look of frustration passes over her face.

She doesn't mention the sleepover again. And I don't tell her anything.

The first bell of the morning rings, signaling that school will be starting very soon.

"We should get to homeroom," I say.

We start walking in that direction, with a big crowd of girls around us now. I keep my secret to myself. And Abby heads to her homeroom without saying another word.

8:05 a.m. Our fifth-grade class has forty-seven girls in it. At the beginning of the year we had forty-eight. We're divided into four different homeroom groups, so there are twelve girls in each homeroom, except for ours. We only have eleven.

Abby's not in my homeroom this year. But Sloane is. So I take a deep breath and try to compose myself before heading into the classroom where my group meets.

At our school, homeroom isn't just a place to go at the beginning of the day. It's supposed to be a place where we can ask questions, talk about problems, and share feelings. This is where we talk about things like puberty and violence in the news and online bullying. It's supposed to be a safe space. A home, at school.

But with a girl like Sloane in the room, it isn't. I'm not the only one who thinks so.

On the second day of school this year—which seems like a really, really long time ago—a girl named Eleanor, who had just moved to San Francisco from New York City, shared that she was feeling homesick, and that she missed her friends from her old school.

I felt sorry for her. I know it would be hard to start at a new school without Abby. I asked Eleanor to sit with us at lunch that day. A lot of people joined us. Eleanor was funny and smart, and I was glad she was going to be in our class.

Sloane wasn't glad. I don't really know why she did what she did—maybe because Eleanor was great and people were starting to like her and even Madison said something about how cool Eleanor was. Anyway, Sloane went around telling everyone that Eleanor hated our school and everyone in it. And then apparently she posted a bunch of really mean and not true things about Eleanor to a fake account on social media—I don't know the details, because I don't have a phone or any social media, and neither does Abby—and it got around to everyone who does have a phone. Not everyone believed it, but Eleanor's parents were furious and they moved her to a different school.

And somehow, Sloane didn't get in trouble.

Apart from all that, she makes everyone feel un-comfortable, with her mean looks and snarky comments and eye rolls—which she's very careful to make sure no teacher ever sees. To teachers' faces, she's all smiles and sympathy.

But anyone who's made the mistake of sharing something too personal in our homeroom has suffered from Sloane's mocking—and had their secret shared with the rest of the school later.

Basically, Sloane is the kind of kid you never want to be—and ideally, never want to have in your homeroom.

But I'm stuck with her, and our homeroom most definitely does not feel like home.

8:08 a.m. Sure enough, the first person I see when I walk through the door is Sloane. We don't have assigned seats in homeroom. We can sit wherever feels comfortable. Apparently, sitting close to the door, watching everyone who comes in, feels comfortable to Sloane.

She locks eyes with me immediately. "Feeling better?" she asks in a loud, singsongy voice as I'm reaching into my backpack to get my homework folder to turn in. A few people glance curiously at me when they hear that, probably wondering what's wrong.

I don't answer. Trying to talk to Sloane never ends well for me. I drop my homework folder on Mr. Tripp's desk, zip up my backpack as firmly as possible, return it to my back, and grip the straps tightly.

Of course, Sloane notices. As I walk past her to get to a seat, I can feel her eyeing me—and my backpack.

It's a trend this year at our school for fifth graders to carry messenger bags. But even before everything happened, there's no way my parents were going to buy me a new bag just because it was trendy.

Besides, I think a backpack is more comfortable for walking.

Sloane, of course, has messenger bags in every color.

My backpack is black, which Mama picked so it wouldn't show dirt, but even so, it's my fourth year with it and it's looking pretty frayed.

"Nice *backpack*," Sloane says, then mutters, "that you've had since kindergarten."

Again, I don't respond.

"Why do you *always* have it with you? You could leave it in your locker, you know. What's in there, anyway?"

Most girls leave all their stuff in their lockers, which are supposed to be safe. But I'm scared to be away from what little stuff I have.

Besides the homework folder I just turned in, and *Charlie and the Chocolate Factory*, and Gilbert, and the plastic sandwich bag of money, there are my favorite colored pencils, a sketchpad, and copies of a few of my other favorite books—*Anne of Green Gables*, *Charlotte's Web*, *Ghost*, and *Wonder*. I couldn't even come close to fitting all my books in here, and choosing which to keep was almost impossible.

I also have a picture of my family—Mama, Daddy, Gabby, and me—and a note my dad left for me a few days before his accident. All it says is *I love you, my Maya*. But as long as I have it, folded tightly and tucked into an inside pocket, I feel like we're connected.

In other words, there's some important stuff in this backpack.

I have to be careful with it.

8:09 a.m. Mr. Tripp happens to be looking the other way, so Sloane quickly reaches out, grabs the zipper of my backpack, and tries to unzip it.

I jerk it away from her. "Don't touch it," I say.

She smirks at me and gives my backpack one more look. Mr. Tripp glances our way, and Sloane sits back with an innocent look on her face.

I choose a seat as far away from Sloane as possible and stow my backpack under the desk, holding it tightly between my feet.

No one unzips this bag but me.

8:15 a.m. The second bell rings, which means everyone should be in homeroom by now. If you walk in after the bell, technically you're supposed to go to the office to let them know you should be marked tardy. But Mr. Tripp is pretty laid-back. Sophy and Sadie walk in about thirty seconds late, and he doesn't send them to the office. They're twins. They're both really nice, although I almost never see them outside of school because they live in South San Francisco, which is pretty far away. They slide into their seats as quickly as they can.

"Good morning, girls," Mr. Tripp says. "Now that you've all graced us with your presence"—he pauses for a second to give Sophy and Sadie a smirk, but it's a friendly one—"we can get started. It's Friday, so we're free-forming it. Who has something on her mind, or anything to share this morning?"

Sophy and Sadie look at each other with huge smiles, then announce at almost exactly the same time, "Our mom is going to have a baby!"

"Wow," says Mr. Tripp. "That is major news. Congratulations to the big sisters!"

Then he adds, with a sly smile, "I still expect you to be on time to homeroom, you know."

"We will," they say at the same time, still grinning.

I happen to know this is extra-good news for their family. A little more than a year ago, their mom was expecting, but she lost the baby soon after they found out about it. And they were all so sad. I have a feeling that this time is going to be different, and I'm really happy for them.

"That's amazing," I say to Sophy, who's sitting closer to me than Sadie is. "Being a big sister is the best." I remember when Mama was pregnant with Gabby, and how excited I was to hold a tiny baby. And then when Gabby arrived, her little hands and feet and face were tinier and cuter than I'd ever imagined they could be.

"That's amazing," Sloane mimics. *"Being a big sister is the best."* And then she adds, "If this baby ever even gets to be born."

The part where she mocked what I said doesn't bother me, although it certainly isn't nice, but my jaw drops when she says the second thing. How can anyone be that mean? I feel anger well up inside, and tears prick the back of my eyes again.

I don't want to look at her, but I can't help it. When I do, she's rolling her eyes at Madison. I'm not sure how mean Madison would be if she had different friends, but she's definitely decided she's on Team Sloane. "Yeah. Like a baby is *soooo* exciting," Madison replies, making sure Mr. Tripp can't hear—but Sophy, Sadie, and I can.

And then Sloane comments, "My father says he doesn't understand why families who can't afford the kids they already have keep having more."

She says it quietly. But it's loud enough for Sophy and Sadie and a few other girls sitting nearby to hear.

Madison responds, but I don't hear what she says. Then they both look at the three of us and giggle.

8:20 a.m. No one else in homeroom has anything to share. Big surprise, after what Sloane just did. Even the kids who didn't hear exactly what she said know she must have said *something*.

I almost never speak up in homeroom anymore, because I never know how Sloane will respond if I do. Earlier in the year I didn't care as much about Sloane, but these days I feel like I'm on the verge of tears almost all the time. And I can't take any extra meanness in the morning. I wonder if I should tell Mr. Tripp what Sloane and Madison just did. They shouldn't be able to get away with that. But I'm not sure I can handle whatever they'll do to me if they realize I've told.

Before I can decide whether or not to tell him, Mr. Tripp starts making an announcement.

"If no one has anything else to share," he says, "it's my turn. The seventh graders have a field trip next Thursday, so we're switching food pantry dates with them. We'll be volunteering there next week, and they'll go on our day later in the year. So we'll be talking about food insecurity and homelessness starting on Monday."

Suddenly I have the sensation of bugs crawling up

my neck. My face is burning. It feels like everyone is staring at me. I don't look around to see if anyone is.

I cannot believe this is happening now. Usually fifth graders volunteer in May, so I didn't think I'd have to worry about it for a while.

It's not that I don't want to help. I do.

I've always liked working at the pantry. Well, except for one part of our work day there last year, when we were in Ms. Rodriguez's fourth-grade class. There was a terrible moment when Sloane and Madison started making fun of an elderly woman who was getting food from the pantry.

The woman didn't want the food item Sloane and Madison were handing out. And she couldn't speak English, and they couldn't understand why she didn't want it. They kept trying to force it on her instead of just letting her move on. And she got upset. "Wow. *She's* a little picky," I heard Sloane say. "Um, *yeah*. She should take what she can get," Madison added. And then they whispered and giggled.

I was at a nearby station with Abby, and I saw the whole thing. There was a flash of sadness and confusion on the woman's face, and then she shuffled to the next station with her head down.

Watching this made me feel like I'd been punched in the stomach. But I didn't know what to do. As I was thinking about whether I should say something and what I should say, Abby spoke up without hesitating. "You guys, stop it," she hissed at them, trying to be quiet enough that the clients of the pantry wouldn't hear but forceful enough that Sloane and Madison would take notice.

"I think you just made her really sad," I added in a whisper.

"If you do that again, I'm going to tell Ms. Rodriguez," Abby said.

Madison and Sloane rolled their eyes, but they stopped. Abby looked at me and shook her head like she couldn't believe what had just happened. And then Sloane whispered something to Madison under her breath, and they both looked at Abby and me and smirked. I tried not to care what they were saying. Abby and I went back to work handing out celery and sweet potatoes, and that was that.

I don't even want to think about what Sloane and Madison would say to me if they knew where I'm living now. Or that we get food from a pantry, too.

8:22 a.m. "I'll remind you about this at the end of the day," Mr. Tripp adds, "but we will also be having a mini canned food drive next week. No one is obligated to donate, but if you have spare cans of beans or soup or vegetables at home, or your family can pick some up at the store, we'd love to collect them so we can make a class donation for the homebound seniors in the neighborhood who can't make it to the pantry."

Thinking about the homebound seniors who get food from the pantry delivered—who can't afford to buy food *and* can't get around the city by themselves—makes me forget for a moment about the weirdness of working at a pantry. I decide that no matter what, I'm going to figure out a way to donate to the food drive. Even if it's the least-expensive can of beans I can find, I'll use some of my $17.32 to buy it.

Sloane isn't thinking about it quite the same way, apparently. "Don't worry," she says to Sophy and Sadie. "You're not *obligated* to donate food if your family can't even afford enough to feed yourselves." Maybe I should be relieved that she's targeting someone other than me, for a change, but it feels worse to hear her say mean things to someone else. This time I'm going to speak up. I raise my hand. Sloane sees me do it. Her eyes narrow as she gives me a look of pure hatred.

But I don't have to say anything, because Mr. Tripp beats me to it.

"What was that, Sloane?" he asks, looming over her desk. I lower my hand. She hadn't realized he was within earshot. At least she has the decency to look embarrassed, which is surprising.

"Oh, I—I was just saying I think I'll be able to bring in a lot of cans for the drive," she stammers, all traces of her teenager voice gone. Maybe she has some feelings in there, somewhere.

Mr. Tripp gives her a long stare and then says, "Well. That would be wonderful. Thank you, Sloane." Then he tells us we can talk quietly or read until it's time for first period.

8:23 a.m. As I wait for the next six and half minutes to tick by while Sloane shoots me looks so nasty that they give me chills, the girls in our homeroom chat about weekend plans, all thoughts of food insecurity and can drives forgotten.

Madison is having a birthday party. I'm not invited. And even though she isn't supposed to talk about it at school, she does. So everyone knows she's pretending it's her "golden birthday," even though it's not.

A golden birthday happens when the age you're turning matches the day of the month—turning eight on the eighth, or twelve on the twelfth. And for many girls who go to my school, golden birthdays tend to mean an over-the-top celebration. Even more over-the-top than usual, that is. I've been to regular birthday celebrations that involved things like celebrity guest chefs, entire blow-dry salons rented out for twelve second graders, and stretch limos to front-row seats at sports games and concerts.

Of course, not everyone's golden birthday happens during elementary or middle school. If you were born on, say, the first day of the month, or the twenty-eighth, you're out of luck. Madison's real golden birthday happened when she was three, but she didn't know about golden birthdays then.

And because that didn't seem fair to her, she's getting a golden birthday celebration now, when she's turning eleven.

I heard that this year her birthday party is going to have an escape room, a cooking competition in the kitchen of a famous restaurant in San Francisco, and a sleepover at a hotel. For twenty girls.

My real golden birthday is coming up in March. I'll be eleven on March 11. I know I won't be getting a fancy birthday celebration at a hotel, but that's not what I want.

More than anything, I just wish I could have dinner with my whole family. And Abby, too.

At home.

8:26 a.m. The conversation around me shifts from this weekend to February break. Which, Ainsley notes with excitement, starts one week from today, after school.

I get a sinking feeling in my stomach. I didn't think it

was possible to feel worse than I already did this morning. Turns out, it is.

February break. Somehow I forgot that February break is coming up so soon. We're one week away from February break.

Oh no.

I try to ignore my creeping sense of dread and tune in to some of the chatter around me. Chiara says she's going skiing at Squaw. Ainsley says she's going skiing in Aspen. Madison says she's going skiing in Sun Valley. None of this is a surprise. A lot of people call winter break "ski week." That used to be the official name of it, but some families and teachers got it changed. Which makes sense. Not everyone skis. And it's ridiculous to name a break for everyone after a kind of trip that not everyone can (or even wants to) take.

Sloane, recovered from her moment of humility, tells them all that she wouldn't bother with Tahoe or Aspen or Sun Valley. She's going to a private ski resort in Montana.

Of course she is. She names the celebrities who also ski there.

A short silence follows Sloane's announcement. No one wants to say anything else about skiing. Finally Noelle pipes up to say that her family is going to a fancy resort in Mexico. She starts to explain why she's more excited to go to the beach than she would be to go skiing, but Sloane stares her down, and she stops short.

Sophy and Sadie don't say anything about where they're going. Neither do some of the other kids. Neither do I, obviously. We're the kids who aren't going anywhere. There's nothing glamorous or cool about saying that, even if we do live in a city that lots of people love to visit on vacation. Last year during break, even though Mama took me on hikes and to museums and even to a trampoline park, I was disappointed that my family always had to stay home when other people got to travel.

It felt kind of boring to wake up at home every single morning of break.

But now I'd give anything just to stay home.

4

ART TiMe

Do what you love.

—*HENRY DAVID THOREAU*

8:30 a.m. The bell rings, and it's time for me to head to art class. Sloane and Madison are lingering just inside the door of our homeroom, whispering. I don't care what they're whispering about, and I'm not waiting for them to leave. I clutch my backpack straps and hurry past them. Because I don't want to miss a second of art.

And not just because Sloane isn't in the class.

All fifth- and sixth-grade art classes are held in a cool studio with huge windows and lots of light, even on a cloudy day like this one. I think it's the best room at our school. And it's where Mama taught when she was the art teacher here.

I'm hoping so hard that Mama's interview goes well today and she gets to teach art again.

Maybe it's not a surprise that art is my favorite subject. (My second favorite is French, and my third favorite is science.) Mama says making art has been my favorite thing to do ever since I was tiny, when I always wanted to scribble with crayons or finger-paint or play with Play-Doh.

We always had lots of art supplies around at my house. We couldn't take most of them with us to the shelter. But I kept a few favorites, in my backpack.

When I'm drawing or painting or making a collage, it's like the world stands still, but time flies by. I don't think about anything else. I just focus on what I'm doing. Even these days, when I have a hard time not thinking about my dad and the shelter and what's going to happen to my family, I can get lost in an art project.

After my dad's accident, I felt guilty about that for a while. It didn't seem fair that I got to make art while he couldn't do anything. When I told Mama that, she just asked, "Maya, do you think he would want you to stop making art? To stop doing something that makes you so happy?"

I know he wouldn't. It's okay for me to keep making art, and loving it.

To get to the art studio from my homeroom, I have

to walk across an outdoor courtyard. As I do, I glance up at the sky. It's getting darker and grayer by the second. And then I walk into the bright, warm art studio.

I look around and feel like I can really breathe for the first time all morning.

Girls are filing in around me, chattering away, but I'm quiet. Some of the signs Mama and the girls in her classes made when she was the art teacher are still here. A many-colored, paint-splattered poster, signed by all the girls in Mama's sixth-grade class a few years ago, proclaims WELCOME, EVERYONE. EVERYONE WELCOME. A huge sign above the welcome sign says, in crooked, mismatched letters that look really cool together, MISTAKES ARE BEAUTIFUL.

Oh, I hope Mama gets the new job so she can teach art again. I hope, I hope, I hope.

There are newer signs here, too. One says THERE IS NO PERFECT. Another says BE HERE NOW. That last one didn't make sense to me at first, because, well, where else would we be? But our art teacher, Ms. Sherman, explained that it means to be fully present in the space where you are at the moment. To pay attention, to soak it up, and not to be thinking about where you're going next or all the other things going on in your life. I like that.

My shoulders relax and my grip on my backpack loosens as I read the signs. Nothing at all is perfect. I make mistakes a lot. But right now, I'm here, in a place I love, a place where Mama used to teach.

In a way, it feels like home.

8:35 a.m. Fortunately, Ms. Sherman, who replaced Mama when she started staying home with Gabby, agrees with Mama's art philosophies and kept her signs on the walls. I love Ms. Sherman. Besides being a teacher, she has her own artwork in shows sometimes. Her paintings are big, colorful, abstract, and happy.

It looks like we won't be painting today. That's okay, because right now Ms. Sherman is cutting clay into big sections for us to use, and the pottery wheels, which are usually covered in the corner of the room, are uncovered and spread out a bit in the studio. I realize that this is the day when we finally get to try making wheel-thrown pottery. That might be the one thing I'm more excited about than painting.

Ms. Sherman is wearing faded jeans, paint-splattered sneakers, and a T-shirt with a peace sign on it. Her long hair has a purple streak on one side, and it's pulled into a bun. She has a short apron on, but I know she's not too worried about getting messy. In fact, one of the signs she added to the art room says PLEASE MAKE A MESS! (JUST CLEAN IT UP WHEN YOU'RE DONE.)

Ms. Sherman is not the kind of art teacher who would ever hold up an example of what a project is "supposed" to look like. She wants us to learn techniques for using different media and then be as creative as we want to be. She teaches us about lots of different artists, especially women who had to fight to make art. And she refuses to say whether a piece of art is good or bad, although girls are constantly showing her artwork and asking her, "Is it good?"

"It's *art*," she always says. "And art is wonderful."

Unless, that is, someone obviously hasn't put any effort into a project. Even then, she won't say something is bad. But she will ask, "Did you give it your all?"

That's something she's asked me only once. It was our first art class after New Year's Day, and my family had just moved out of our house and into the shelter. I couldn't concentrate on anything. Not even art.

We were drawing small, ordinary objects that day. A paper clip, a pencil, a book, a pear, a teacup. But every single small, ordinary object reminded me of all we'd left behind, and that we pretty much didn't have small, ordinary objects anymore.

The idea was to notice all the tiny little details in these simple things. And I tried, but I just couldn't seem to do it. I made a halfhearted sketch of a pear and then stared out the window.

Ms. Sherman walked by and saw my sketch, and saw

that I'd stopped drawing. "Maya, did you give this your all?" she asked, surprised. And then she saw my face.

"Hey," she said kindly. "Is everything okay?"

I remember not being able to speak. I shook my head and fought back tears.

"Everything's not okay. Did something happen . . . ?" She didn't finish the thought, but I knew what she was thinking. She was wondering if something had changed with my dad.

"He's the same," I whispered.

"Okay," she said quietly. "Do you want to talk about what else is going on?"

"Not now," I said.

"Okay," she said again, and paused. She put her hand gently on my shoulder. "But if you ever do, I'm here. Deal?"

I nodded.

She didn't fix anything by checking in with me that day. But by noticing, and caring, she made me feel just a tiny bit better, and less alone.

And I've been mostly able to pay attention—in art class, at least—ever since.

8:36 a.m. Everyone has arrived—there are only twelve girls in this class, because it's an elective—and Ms.

Sherman claps her hands together. "Okay, girls, come join me at a wheel," she says.

We form a half circle around one of the potter's wheels, and Ms. Sherman explains that we're going to attempt bowl-making. "Has anyone ever used one of these wheels before?" she asks.

Aisha raises her hand. "I tried it at camp at the Y last summer," she says. "It's kind of hard."

"But isn't it also kind of cool?" asks Ms. Sherman.

"Yeah, it is," Aisha says, smiling.

"Very cool," says Ms. Sherman. "But you're right, Aisha—it's not easy. And since for most of you this will be the first time you're trying it, just go with the flow and see what happens. You'll have plenty of time to try and try and try again today, and we'll do this a few more times over the next few weeks. Sound good?"

"Sounds good," a few of us say.

"Good!" Ms. Sherman says. "Now, here's how you get started. By the way, making a bowl this way is called throwing a bowl. So if you ever feel so frustrated that you want to throw a bowl, try this." She grins at us, then gets to work.

She shows us how to throw the slab of clay onto the wheel and center it, using water to keep our hands wet so the clay moves easily. She starts shaping the slab of clay into a cylinder as the wheel keeps spinning. Then she starts moving her hands slowly to shape the clay into a bowl.

"Patience is key," she says. "Small movements make a big difference. And if things don't go quite how you want them to . . ."

She intentionally presses too hard on one side of the clay, and the wall of her bowl collapses. She lets the wheel stop spinning and gathers up the clay, then continues her train of thought.

". . . you've probably learned something in the process. And guess what? You can start over as many times as you'd like."

8:45 a.m. I've used clay before, making pinch pots and coil pots and hand-shaped plates. But I've never used a pottery wheel. Watching the clay spin around and around is soothing. I want to know what it feels like.

There are twelve pottery wheels in the art studio, so everyone has her own. This is lucky. Not every school has this kind of art studio. I choose a wheel at the far edge of the room instead of one in the middle of everything. When I'm making any kind of art, I like my space to be quiet and calm.

This wasn't easy in our little house with Gabby around, but it has been way harder in the shelter.

There's no good surface in our shelter room for drawing or painting. I can draw in my sketchbook while I'm sitting on my mattress, but the room is *tiny* and Mama and Gabby are right there. Our shelter does have an arts and crafts room for kids, which is pretty cool, I guess. But it's not very big, and it's usually filled with little kids all competing for the glitter glue. It can be pretty loud and chaotic.

Our shelter also has a playroom, with some old toys and a few kids' books and a game table. That's usually crowded, too. Kids living in a shelter need to get out of their rooms, and there's nowhere else to go.

I'm glad they have those spaces where we can see other kids. It makes living in a shelter feel less lonely. Not that I want other people to have to live there, but somehow it feels better knowing I'm not the only kid going through this.

I've even made some friends there. And I've learned that kids in shelters all have different stories. Really hard stories. Some have slept on the streets. Some had to leave their house because of violence. Some had to leave their whole *country* because of violence. Some don't think they'll ever have a home again.

My closest friend at the shelter is Haya. She's also ten, although she just turned ten and she's in fourth grade. She's one of seven kids, and they're all at the shelter with her dad. They moved to the United States from Yemen three years ago. And then her mom got really sick, and she hasn't gotten better. Like my dad, Haya's mom is in the hospital, and they're not sure if she's going to make it.

Haya's dad is a rideshare driver, but without her mom around to watch the kids, he hasn't been able to drive enough to make enough money to keep paying rent. And so they lost their apartment. They moved to the shelter about two weeks before we did.

I met Haya when we were both looking for some quiet space among all the little kids. I wanted to draw, and she wanted to practice chess. She's really good at chess, and there's an old chessboard in the playroom.

I've never played chess so I didn't understand how she could play by herself, but she said she could study the board and practice different match strategies. When we get lucky, we find an empty table to share. I draw and she fiddles around with chess pieces and we don't talk much.

But we're together.

Haya told me a few days ago that the times when we're together and when she's studying chess are some of the only times when she doesn't feel like crying.

I know how she feels.

8:47 a.m. Making art can mostly distract me from that feeling of wanting to cry. When Ms. Sherman hands me a section of clay, I stop thinking about anything else.

I knead it a bit, then throw it on the wheel. I wet my hands, shape it into a cylinder, and begin to play.

For the next hour, my hands get covered with clay as I experiment with different techniques and strategies and pressures, start over at least a dozen times, and finally create something that resembles an actual bowl.

9:53 a.m. I haven't paid attention to what any of the other girls are making. And I don't think anyone has paid attention to me. In art, that's how I like it. Ms. Sherman checked in as I was making my first few attempts, but she knows that when I get going on an art project, I like to lose myself in it.

She does come over when she notices my raised hand. I'm not sure how to get my best bowl off the pottery wheel without denting it. As she comes close to my wheel, her eyes open wide. In a good way.

"Wow, Maya," she says. "You're really getting it." She smiles.

"Thanks," I say. "But . . . what do I do with it now?"

"This looks like a keeper to me. What do you think?" she says.

It flashes through my mind that I don't actually have a place to keep it, but I let that go. I like the bowl. I do want to keep it.

"It's a keeper," I agree.

"So I'm glad you didn't try to take it off without a tool," she says. "Actually, everyone should watch this. Hey, girls," she calls. "Take a break for a sec and watch what to do if you have a bowl you want to keep."

All the girls look up from their wheels. "Wow. Nice, Maya," says Aisha.

"Yeah, wow. That's great," Ellie agrees.

"Oh, so *that's* what it's supposed to look like," Vivi says, glancing back at her own bowl and laughing. "That's awesome."

"Thanks," I say. At first I try not to smile, but the smile inside wants to come out, so I let it. The girls in this class are kind. And compliments feel good. It's okay to smile when you get one.

Ms. Sherman takes a wire from the tool rack and carefully slides it under my bowl to separate it from the wheel. Then she gently lifts the bowl from the bottom and holds it up so I can scratch my initials into the bottom. She sets it on a high rack, where I know it will be safe until she can fire it in the kiln.

I find myself wishing there were a safe, high shelf where I could put myself to get away from everything and just rest for a while.

10:00 a.m. I'm slow to leave the art studio. I don't want to go. I won't have art again until next Friday.

Next Friday is also the last day of school before winter break. Nine straight days with no school. Nine straight days with nowhere to go but the shelter or the hospital.

I'm in no rush to get to next Friday.

My next class is science, and the classroom is upstairs from the art studio. But what's cool about this building is that the stairs are outside. And as you're climbing up them, you can see out to the Pacific Ocean and the Golden Gate Bridge, unless it's foggy and the bridge is totally hidden.

The sky is gray and getting grayer today, but we aren't completely fogged in, so I can see part of the bridge. But it's impossible to see all the way to the other side. I suppose anyone trying to cross it right now just has to believe there's something there.

10:01 a.m. Our science teacher, Dr. Spalding, is super smart and very cool. Dr. Spalding is gender non-conforming, so instead of saying "him" or "her" or "he" or "she," we say "they" or "them" or just "Doc."

What I love most about Doc's class is that we don't just study a topic—like, say, the digestive system or making circuits. We always talk about how it relates to the world, and how science can make the world a better place.

For the past several classes we've been designing and building solar ovens and talking about why using solar power instead of fossil fuels for energy is so important for the planet. On the first sunny day after they're done, we get to use them to make nachos and s'mores.

I wish I could have a snack like that right now. After skipping breakfast, I'm starting to get really hungry. But number one, it's not sunny, and number two, I'm not sure everyone in our class has finished making sure their ovens are built to maximize internal temperature (that is, get as hot inside as possible).

I try not to think about how hungry I am and instead wonder what Doc is going to talk about today. I almost always leave Doc's class feeling inspired about doing good in the world. Doc reminds me of my dad in that way. My dad was always thinking about how things—the food we eat, the things we buy, the way we get around—are connected and important. And how we can make the world better. My dad was a huge fan of Doc. And so am I.

So I'm feeling almost excited as I approach my science classroom. But I guess that good feeling is not meant to last. Not today.

Because guess who's just outside the science room door.

10:02 a.m. I'm not even sure why she's there, because she isn't in my science class. But of course it's Sloane.

She's standing and whispering with Lucy, who *is* in my science class. Although she still ignores me when Sloane is around, Lucy is almost tolerable when Sloane *isn't* around, so having her in my class doesn't bother me.

Except now, when she's hanging out with Sloane. Couldn't they think of any better place to go?

Sloane stops whispering when she sees me. She stares, then smirks.

"What's all over your jumper, Maya?" she asks.

I look down. I got some clay on it during art. Oh well. It's none of her business what it is.

My plan is to ignore the question and head straight into science, but Sloane shifts slightly so she's partly blocking the doorway.

"Seriously, Maya, what *is* that?" she asks. "Did you have some kind of . . . *accident*? That's disgusting." She snickers and looks at Lucy, who looks at her blankly, not getting the joke.

I think Sloane was suggesting I had some sort of bathroom accident and got it on my jumper, but come on. That's a stretch, even for Sloane. It doesn't look like that at all. No wonder Lucy's confused.

Still, if I seem embarrassed or hesitant, I know I'll never hear the end of this, and the rumor will spread all over fifth grade. So now I do respond.

"It's clay, Sloane," I say, flatly and firmly, then slide past her into the classroom.

"*Sure* it is," I hear her say. Lucy murmurs something back that I don't hear.

"Well, at least it goes with all the other stains on her jumper. So gross. Hasn't her family ever heard of, like, a *washing machine?*" Sloane adds, directing her question to Lucy.

It's such a stupid insult. And yet it feels like a knife twisting in me. *Yes, we know what a washing machine is!* I want to scream. *But we don't have one in our homeless shelter! How many do you have in your two giant mansions?*

I don't, though. I don't have the energy.

And then something surprising happens. Lucy simply shrugs and follows me into science. I can't believe she didn't take the bait and respond with a snide comment of her own.

Sloane is suddenly left alone. I'm sure she wants to say something else, but without an audience, she doesn't. She stares after Lucy, looking confused and a little hurt. She's used to people behaving exactly the way she wants them to. That didn't happen this time. So she heads off toward her class, head down.

Then Lucy shocks me by whispering, "I can tell it's clay. I have no idea what she was talking about with that accident thing. Sorry she's so . . . um . . . you know . . . to you . . ." Lucy trails off. And I remember for a second what it was like to be friends with her.

I give her a half smile. I take the high road and don't say anything about Sloane. "If you have art class later, you'll probably get to play with clay, too," I say.

"Nice," she says, and turns toward the front of the room, where Doc is getting ready to start class.

10:05 a.m. "I have good news and bad news," says Doc as the last of the chatter quiets down. "The good news is that your solar ovens are awesome. They're just about ready to go. They're going to cook some killer nachos and s'mores.

"But that isn't going to happen today, unfortunately."

Several girls groan. Violet even whines, "Why *not?*"

Doc laughs. "Anyone care to explain why not? And by the way, you know there's no whining in science."

Several hands shoot into the air. Not mine, though. I know the answer, of course, but right now even a simple explanation like that feels daunting. I'm tired, I'm hungry, and I'm worn out. And we're only about halfway through the school morning.

Doc calls on Lily, who smiles and points out the window, where the sky is growing darker by the minute. "We're missing something," she says. "Sun, anyone?"

"Right," Doc says. "And speaking of weather . . ."

Doc launches into a discussion of weather and

climate change, which we talk about a lot. But each time we cover it, we build on what we've learned and go deeper.

Doc also tells us that after winter break we're going to be working in teams on plans for climate change solutions. Aside from the reminder about winter break coming up, that sounds good to me. This class is always so interesting that I really, really want to tune in. When I'm as wiped out as I am most days, it's really easy to zone out in a boring class. But science class flies by, and before I know it, Doc is telling us to have a great weekend.

10:50 a.m. "Cross your fingers and wish for sun on Monday," Doc says.

I cross my fingers and wish for sun—and while I'm at it, I make wishes for Mama and my dad, too—before grabbing my backpack and heading out the door.

5

BReAK TiMe

Keep good company,
read good books, love good things.

—LOUISA MAY ALCOTT

10:51 a.m. Now we get a fifteen-minute free period between classes. Our teachers still call it recess, but for most of the girls in fifth grade, it doesn't look much like the recess I loved when I was in kindergarten and first grade. Back then, we used to climb on the monkey bars and build forts with big foam blocks and play Four Square and chase each other around the playground. I wish it were still like that every day. But mostly people just sit around and talk.

I like talking to Abby, and to Sophy and Sadie and Aisha and Vivi and Ellie and Lily, and sometimes we do just talk, but those girls will also get up and play. Sometimes we play soccer or basketball or tetherball, and sometimes we play tag with the first graders, who are our school "little sisters."

Sloane calls us babies when we do this—but we don't care. The first graders love it when older girls play with them. And honestly, it's fun for us, too. Much more fun than sitting around talking about clothes or YouTube or TikTok or trying to sneak a peek at someone's phone.

But today I'm heading to recess alone. The first graders are on a field trip to the San Francisco Symphony. Abby, Vivi, Ellie, and Lily have to finish a project in our school's tinker lab—they all take a STEM elective together. And every Friday there's an affinity group meeting for students of color, so that's where Sophy, Sadie, and Aisha are. They've told me it helps them to talk about the experiences they have not being white at a school where the majority of students are. They say people make comments and treat them in ways that I might not notice but that hurt their feelings. Little phrases that might seem harmless on the surface but aren't harmless at all. And then there are the more obvious comments that anyone can tell would be hurtful. I've heard plenty of those directed at them, too.

I know it's not the same, but I've been wondering lately if it's a little bit like how I feel when someone makes an offhand comment about a second home or expensive new clothes, or laughs at someone's used uniform or old shoes. They're showing off about a privilege that they don't even realize they have.

I take a few steps toward the upper-school courtyard and playground and right away see Sloane and Madison and Lucy. They're inseparable at recess, usually glued to Sloane's phone. I'm pretty sure Sloane would throw a fit if one of them tried to hang out with someone else.

I know there are some nice girls out there, too, somewhere beyond Sloane and her crew. But I don't have the energy to find them.

I need a safe space. And I know where to find one.

10:52 a.m. I turn around and head to the school library. I open the door and leave the cold gray air behind. Inside it's warm and bright, just like I knew it would be. I breathe in the smell of books.

I go straight to the lower-school library. Upper-school girls (that's fifth through eighth graders at my school) are allowed to go in there as long as we don't interfere with a lower-school class. I know there aren't any classes in there right now—there never are during morning recess on Fridays—and lower-school girls aren't allowed to come in on their own during recess except on Wednesdays. So it shouldn't be crowded.

In fact, I have it all to myself. That surprises me, because on a cold, gray day like this one, I can't think of anywhere better to go. And I don't know why everyone doesn't take shelter in here.

I head to a shelf of middle-grade chapter books and quickly find the Ramona series. These have been some of my favorite books since I started reading them in first grade. Ramona seems *real,* and her family, like mine, has problems and not much money.

In third grade, my teacher Ms. Banks talked about the idea of "comfort reading," which is basically reading any book that makes you feel like you're wrapped in a warm blanket. And she recommended comfort reading anytime we were having a bad day. It was good advice.

Ramona is definitely comfort reading for me. I didn't have space in my backpack for the whole series, so I left it behind. I knew my library had them all.

I skip *Ramona and Her Father* because it would make me too sad. That's the one where Ramona's father loses his job and the family is more worried about money than usual. It reminds me of my family.

Even when we had a house, we were always thinking about saving money. We didn't buy anything we didn't need. Gabby and I wore hand-me-downs. I got my school clothes from the used-uniform sale instead of buying them new. Our family shopped for food at a farmers' market that sold organic vegetables and fruit labeled "cosmetically challenged" for really low prices. When I first noticed the sign that said that, I didn't know what it meant, but Mama laughed and told me it was a funny way to say that the fruit didn't look perfect but it was still perfectly good to eat. It always tasted delicious to me, especially when my dad cooked. Before he became a writer, he worked in a restaurant. He started as a line cook and worked his way up to being a sous-chef (the second-in-command to the head chef) before he left to write full-time. He got really, really good at cooking—so no matter how tight money was, he always made something yummy. We haven't had much yummy food lately.

In *Ramona and Her Father*, Ramona gets to spend a lot of time with her dad, and I know it would make me think about all the time I used to spend with *my* dad. I wonder if he'll be able to remember any of that, when he wakes up.

Instead I grab *Ramona the Brave*. I'm sure if Sloane and her friends saw me reading a book about a first grader, they'd make fun of me, but I don't care. Besides, they never come into the library unless they have to.

I get lost in Ramona's problems: her classmates not believing her story at show-and-tell; a girl who copies her owl design for an art project; being scared to sleep alone in her new room. The bell rings and I smile, thinking that at least sleeping alone isn't something I have to worry about these days. There's something cozy about sleeping so close to Mama and Gabby. Maybe if we weren't going through all this, I wouldn't need it, but right now I do. It makes me feel safer and better, being near people I love.

Reading about Ramona has made me feel a little better, too, and I think I'm ready to face people again.

6

FReNCH TiMe

L'essentiel est invisible pour les yeux.
(What is essential is invisible to the eye.)

—ANTOINE DE SAINT-EXUPÉRY

11:05 a.m. Our school doesn't have many indoor hallways, and to get just about anywhere at my school, I have to go outside. As I walk to French class, I look up at the sky. It's getting darker, and the airs smells like metal.

The rain is coming.

No one is paying as much attention as I am to the weather. Because everyone else has a raincoat and a home with a hot shower and a washer and dryer. And plenty of them also have designer rain boots in a rainbow of colors and will be picked up from school in huge cars with heated seats. But I know that once I'm wet in this chilly weather, it may be a long time before I'm truly warm again.

At least I'm not wet yet, and the small classroom where Madame Herbert—we usually just call her Madame—teaches French is cozy. Better yet, Abby is in my class. (Sloane is, too, but with Abby there, it's not so bad.) Abby and I usually arrive as early as we can so we can choose seats next to each other—there's no assigned seating in French—and maybe have a few minutes to talk. But today when I arrive, Abby's not there. She doesn't come until Madame is starting class. Abby slides into a seat near the door without looking at me, no matter how much I try to make eye contact. She's never done that.

Suddenly the small room feels too hot, and I keep shifting around in my seat, trying to get comfortable. But I can't. I think Abby is mad at me about the sleepover. It takes a lot to make Abby mad, but when she is, she doesn't always get over it quickly. Or at all.

Next time we're alone, I hope I'll be brave enough to explain. I will be, I decide. No matter what. When the decision clicks in my head, I start to breathe more easily and I stop sweating.

On Fridays when we come into French class, we always find a single vocabulary word written on the whiteboard. And then we talk about that word and learn other words related to it. Last week when we came in, the word on the board was *"gentille,"* which means "nice" or "kind." That led to a conversation about kindness and what being kind means to us. And we talked about being *généreuse* ("generous"), *aimable* ("friendly"), and *respectueuse* ("respectful").

During that conversation, I was hoping all the girls were paying attention. I think Madame hoped so, too.

This week it's a different word. As I read it, I sigh and fight back tears for at least the third time this morning, and start shifting around in my seat again.

The word is *"la maison."*

Which means "house," or "home."

11:07 a.m. Madame asks everyone in the class to think of things they associate with home. *En français, si c'est possible.* (In French, if possible.)

Madison raises her hand and asks, in English, "Does this have to be just about our house in San Francisco? Because we have different things in our different houses."

Sloane nods in agreement. "Yeah, like our ski house and our beach house and our house in Napa." She doesn't mention the spare San Francisco house.

I roll my eyes. I don't care if anyone sees. It's too much. Some people have everything and don't even realize that other people have nothing.

I think I see Madame roll her eyes, too, just the tiniest bit, before she responds. "That's not really the point, girls," she explains. "It's more about what you associate with home—with the feeling of being at home. Okay. Any words to share?"

"*Les vêtements!*" Noelle exclaims happily. "When I'm at home, I don't have to wear this uniform and I can wear anything I want to from my closet. Plus, I have clothes at all my houses."

Madame barely nods and doesn't respond, although I think I hear her sigh. "*D'accord. Quelqu'un d'autre?*" (That means "Okay. Anyone else?") She looks around for other raised hands.

"*La pizza!*" says Lily. "We always have pizza at my house on Friday nights."

"*Délicieuse!*" Madame says. Delicious.

A few months ago, I might have said "*la pizza*," too, when I thought about home on a Friday. Not anymore. But of course now I'm thinking about my family's pizza nights, and one more time I feel the sting of tears behind my eyes. I also feel hungry, thinking about my dad's chewy pizza crust and amazing sauce.

We're still a long way from lunch.

"*Les jeux vidéo,*" says Madison. "Is that how you say 'video games'? And . . . how do you say 'bouncy house' in French? We have video games and a bouncy house in our playroom. And that's my favorite room in our house. Well, the one in San Francisco."

I swear Madame rolls her eyes again. *"Quelqu'un d'autre?"*

Abby raises her hand and says, *"Mon chien!"* That means "my dog." Abby loves her dog. For her, home is where her dog is.

Abby got her dog almost two years ago, when she turned nine. Her birthday is two days before mine, on March 9, so that was her golden birthday. And the only thing she wanted for her golden birthday was a dog.

Specifically, she wanted to adopt a dog from the San Francisco SPCA. She had seen pictures of the dogs available for adoption in the window of the SPCA animal hospital on Fillmore Street. For the most part, they weren't all that cute, and they weren't brand-new puppies. But she wanted one.

I got to go with her to choose one. Her parents had filled out all the paperwork in advance, and we went to the SPCA adoption center in the Mission neighborhood. We stopped for burritos first—the only other birthday request she had that year.

When we got there, Abby wandered around, looking carefully at all the dogs. And then she locked eyes with a small, fluffy gray-and-white dog.

The sign said the dog was a two-year-old Alaskan husky mix, but she must have been mixed with a much smaller dog because the sign outside her cage said she only weighed about twenty-five pounds.

Her coat was pretty patchy, and she looked a little ragged, but I have to admit, there was something adorable about her face. And she was staring at Abby as if she were in love.

I looked at Abby and could see that she'd fallen in love, too. "This is my dog!" she announced, with tears in her eyes. An SPCA volunteer opened the cage. When the dog stood up, we all realized that she was missing one of her back legs.

The man from the SPCA explained that she'd been hit by a car, and her leg had been injured so badly that it had to be amputated. And her former owner didn't want a three-legged dog.

By that point Abby was full-on crying. So was I. I wondered how Abby would respond, but I had a feeling I knew.

"That's crazy!" she said as the dog came toward her and nuzzled her face. "Who wouldn't want this dog?"

And that was that. Abby's *chien*. She named her Marshmallow because she was so fluffy—or looked like she would be, after a good bath and a lot of love.

Madame smiles when she hears Abby mention something that isn't clothes or video games or a vacation house. So do I. *"Quel est le nom de ton chien?"* she asks Abby. Abby pauses, translating the words in her head, and realizes that Madame is asking about her dog's name.

"Oh!" she says. *"Elle s'appelle Marshmallow."*

"Lame dog, stupid name," Sloane says to Madison, then looks at me. She wants to make sure I heard. Madison laughs. I just smile at Abby. She sees me. And I think she even smiles back.

11:22 a.m. I ignore Sloane and think instead about Abby nuzzling Marshmallow's face. And try to come up with my own word. What do I most associate with home? Even if I don't actually have a home? I barely have anything. We don't have a dog or a cat. My backpack is a home for the few things I do have, and many of them remind me of home, but *"sac à dos"* (which means "backpack") wouldn't make sense to anyone but me. And I certainly don't want to explain.

Then the word comes to me.

I raise my hand. Madame points to me. *"Oui, Maya?"*

Out of the corner of my eye, I see Sloane lean forward in her seat, as if she's getting ready to pounce on me the second I say something.

I say it anyway.

"Ma famille."

My family.

That's what home is to me.

I feel so happy about this answer that I don't care what Sloane is going to say. Except—she doesn't say anything. I know she heard what I said, but then she just sank back into her chair. And if I didn't know better, I'd think she looked a little sad.

Madame nods enthusiastically. *"Ta famille,"* she says. *"Oui. C'est belle."* Which means "Yes. That's beautiful."

11:55 a.m Just as French class is ending, I hear it. The pinging sound of the raindrops hitting the roof. And then comes the thundering sound of a total downpour.

I look out the window, and sure enough, rain is coming in torrents. I knew rain was on its way. I just didn't know it would rain quite this hard. Suddenly I feel like I have weights on my shoulders, and like my head weighs a thousand pounds.

The other girls pull on their raincoats. The ones who are wearing those fancy rain boots compare colors.

Abby has a raincoat and a pair of the fancy boots, but I happen to know hers are hand-me-downs from her older cousin. Her family could afford to buy everything new, but they don't when there's perfectly good gear available. She doesn't bother comparing colors. Hers are black. She doesn't really care what color they are.

Abby's next class is science, and she likes to get there as early as possible. So she usually rushes out of the French room. *"Au revoir, Madame,"* she says. She glances at me for just a second, not looking angry anymore. And then she's gone.

It's okay. It will be okay. I just need to talk to her.

As the other girls file out behind Abby, and I walk slowly toward the door, Madame places a gentle hand on my shoulder.

She nods and smiles at me again. *"Ta famille, Maya. Très bien."*

It gives me a warm feeling inside. Maybe that will help me stay warm today.

Even as the icy-cold rain dumps down from the sky.

11:56 a.m. I linger in the doorway of the French classroom for a moment to see if the rain will lighten up. It doesn't. If anything, it gets harder. I'm glad Mama's interview started earlier this morning, so she and Gabby didn't get drenched on their way there. I hope the rain doesn't keep them from getting to the hospital to be with my dad later.

The other girls make their way outside, a few of them

splashing with their tall rain boots in the puddles that are quickly forming.

I'm the last one there, bracing myself for a soaking, when Madame comes up behind me.

"Maya?" she says gently, glancing outside and then at my too-small sweatshirt. *"As-tu un imperméable?"* (She's asking me if I have a raincoat.)

"Ummm, *non,*" I reply, thinking quickly. I'll tell her I forgot it. *"Je l'ai oublié."*

"Voilà," she says. *"Un parapluie pour toi."* And she hands me her umbrella.

"But, Madame . . . ," I say, forgetting to speak French, and she holds up her hand to stop me.

"Pas de problème. J'ai un autre." She's telling me it's no problem, that she has another.

As the rain beats down, I feel a little embarrassed. No one else needs a teacher to lend her an umbrella. But it would be silly to turn it down. So I take it.

"Merci, Madame," I say, taking the umbrella. "I'll bring it back." (I'm not sure how to say that in French.)

She smiles. *"Je sais."* Which means "I know."

11:57 a.m. I step just outside, pop open the umbrella, and cross the courtyard on my way to math class. Although my sneakers and leggings get damp, I'm careful to avoid puddles, and the rest of me stays mostly dry. Rain drips from the edges of the umbrella. All that water would be on me, soaking me, if Madame hadn't noticed that I needed help.

It probably didn't seem like a big deal to her to lend me the umbrella. But it's going to make a huge difference in my day.

Small acts of kindness can do that.

7

TeST TiMe

The best way out is always through.

—ROBERT FROST

11:58 a.m. On my way to math class, I pass a big cypress tree in the courtyard. The lower-school science teacher hung a bird feeder from one of the lower branches, and I usually see birds flying in and out of the tree to eat. But right now there's no bird on the feeder. I pause for a second to look at the tree, and I think I might see one bird moving, way up in the middle of the leaves. But I'm not sure.

And I think about birds for a moment. They don't have a nice warm house to go to, either. So what do they do when it rains?

* * *

12:00 noon Upper-schoolers have the last lunch period of the day, and it doesn't start until almost one o'clock. Math is my last class before lunch. As I slide into my seat, my stomach, which has been grumbling since before science class, starts seriously growling.

I am really, really hungry.

I'm starting to wish I'd taken one of the bananas, but I also hope it helped Gabby this morning. She needs to be in a good mood today.

Mama's interview is for a job she is really excited about. I think she has a good chance of getting it, too. And Gabby is with her at the interview. Mama is an amazing artist and an amazing teacher, but it's not easy for her to get a job. Because she needs to be able to bring a two-and-a-half-year-old to work with her.

Gabby's food allergies are so severe that Mama is afraid to let anyone else feed her. Both times Mama tried dropping Gabby off at a day care, someone gave her something with a trace of the wrong ingredient in it, and Gabby ended up in the emergency room.

So Mama needs a job where she and Gabby can be in the same place, and where Mama can check in at snack time and lunchtime. One solution is a preschool teaching job, but finding one that worked for both of them seemed like it was going to be impossible.

Then, after months of searching, Mama heard about

a preschool looking for a lead art teacher. And it happens to be exactly the kind of school Mama and Daddy want for Gabby. It's all about play and natural materials and creativity. It's perfect. And the director of the school knows all about the situation with Gabby, and still wants to meet with Mama.

That's where they are today. Mama and Gabby are spending a lot of the day at the school. They're there right now.

When they're done, they're going to the hospital. This week, after the tracheostomy procedure, my dad's doctors are weaning him off sedatives—the drugs that have been keeping him asleep while he heals—and today they're hoping he'll be awake enough for the doctors to see if he can breathe on his own. His body needed time to heal before they could do this. Now they want to be able to check his brain function, and they can't while he's sedated. It's all been a mess.

I've been trying not to think too much about that, or worry about Mama's interview, or worry that she's worrying about my dad during her interview. But all of that has never been far from my mind today. And now all of a sudden I can't stop thinking about it.

And then for some reason—maybe because I'm craving s'mores—I remember Doc telling us to cross our fingers and wish for sun. I cross my fingers again under my desk, close my eyes for a second, and make two wishes: that the interview is going well—and that my dad's lungs are healed.

I open my eyes and realize that class has started. And that my math teacher, Mr. Bates, is talking to me.

I haven't heard a word he's said.

12:02 p.m. "Care to join us, Maya?" Mr. Bates asks sarcastically.

Mr. Bates has been teaching at my school for almost forty years. A lot of parents think he shouldn't be here anymore. I've heard them talk about his "outdated methods of communication with students." Right now I would agree with that. But I think he's an okay math teacher.

Sloane, who is in my math class, doesn't miss the opportunity to snicker and whisper something about me falling asleep to her nearest faithful sidekick. In this class, that's Lucy. But Lucy, I notice, doesn't whisper back. So that's something.

I ignore Sloane and keep my response simple. "Yes," I reply. "Can you please repeat the question?"

"It wasn't a question," he snaps. "We are waiting for you to clear your desk so I may distribute the test."

I stare at him. As usual, Mr. Bates's threadbare tie clashes with his rumpled shirt, which clashes with his

V-neck sweater, which has holes in the elbows. Everything he's wearing looks like it might have been around since he started teaching here. Sometimes I hear kids making fun of his outfits. And sure, he could coordinate his colors a little better. But my mom told me his wife has been in and out of the hospital for years. And it has occurred to me lately that he probably has things other than clothes to spend his time and money on.

I can't muster any empathy right now, though. The side of my face feels prickly, and there's a ringing in my ears. *Oh no. Oh no. Oh no.* I thought I was so on top of things. I was so proud of myself for turning in my homework early.

But I completely and totally forgot that we have a math test today.

I grip the edges of my desk. Who was I kidding? I don't have anything together. I'm a mess. I'm exhausted. And right now, I feel utterly overwhelmed.

I didn't study one bit for this test.

12:03 p.m. I've always been a good math student. (I've always been a good everything student.) In math, I'm one of the kids who almost always have the right answer.

It's been hard, though, lately. I'm almost always crazy hungry during math class, and math takes a lot of concentration. Concentrating is extra challenging when you're hungry. Sometimes I get mad—at myself, at the world; I'm not sure which—when I struggle in math just because I haven't eaten enough. But getting mad isn't going to help on this test.

We're doing a geometry unit in math right now, solving problems using the angles and lengths of the sides of triangles and quadrilaterals (that means four-sided shapes) and three-dimensional shapes.

I like geometry because thinking about shapes makes me think about art and architecture. I love drawing and painting buildings, and if you want to do that well, it helps to understand how shapes and angles really work. And I have understood what we've learned in this unit. Even if I forgot there was a test.

I try to calm myself down by breathing slowly. That's one of the tools our teachers are constantly reminding us about when we have SEL (social and emotional learning) every week. And slow, deep breathing usually does help. Unfortunately, it can't change the fact that I didn't study, and it can't make my hunger go away.

I know I'm not the only kid in this city who goes to school hungry. Maybe at my school most kids have plenty to eat, but before his accident my dad talked to us about hunger, and how it, like homelessness, is a huge problem in San Francisco. And that the only real meals lots of kids get are at school. That's not fair.

One of the reasons my dad wanted to work with the

famous chef on her cookbook was because her restaurants are really careful about not wasting food, and they always donate excess food to the homeless and have special dinners to raise funds for child hunger relief organizations.

But now my dad is hooked up to machines in the hospital, and I'm one of the kids going to school hungry.

12:04 p.m. I try to bring my mind back to the present as Mr. Bates drops the test onto my desk. I go back to the slow breathing as I stare at the first problem. Okay. I can do this one. Inhale. Exhale.

I'm going to get through this the only way I can. Slowly and carefully. One problem at a time.

12:50 p.m. I've had to do slow breathing and force myself to stay focused about a hundred times, but I'm working my way through the problems and—I think—doing most of them right. I glance at the clock. There are five minutes left in class, and I have one problem to go. Then Mr. Bates abruptly barks, "Pencils down!"

I look up, surprised. Seriously? He's stopping us five minutes early?

I'm raising my hand to point out the time when I hear Sloane call from the back of the class, "But we have five more minutes!" And I feel weirdly grateful for that, even if she whined it instead of pointing it out politely. But it doesn't help.

"Not on the test, you don't," Mr. Bates replies. "You've had plenty of time to finish."

I know he's not going to change his mind. I'm sure some parents are going to be complaining about this. Probably Sloane's parents. Anyway, I'm not going to finish. But it wasn't the total disaster it could have been.

Mr. Bates collects the tests, then explains our fairly lengthy homework assignment for the weekend. Some teachers give you a little break after a test. Not Mr. Bates.

12:54 p.m. On many days, Mr. Bates keeps us in math class a few minutes longer than he's supposed to. "I decide when you leave," he reminds us if we close our binders before he dismisses us. "Not the clock."

Thankfully, he doesn't do that today. Even before the clock flips to 12:55, he announces, "We're done. Do *not* slack off on your homework. There may be a bonus point on today's test for anyone who gets it all right. And," he adds, "I may feel like a pop quiz on Monday, just to make sure you understand the material." Then he storms out of the room. Maybe he's hoping to beat us all to lunch.

Which makes sense. The food at my school is surprisingly good. And today is pizza day, which is everyone's favorite. Mama says when she was a kid, her school sometimes had pizza day, but it tasted like reheated frozen cardboard. Ours isn't like that. It has a perfectly chewy-crisp crust, yummy sauce, and gooey melty cheese.

Because of Gabby's allergies, the only times I get to eat pizza with regular crust and cheese are when I'm at school and when I go to Abby's house.

That is, when I used to go to Abby's house.

8

LuNCHTiMe

Though much is taken, much abides.

—ALFRED, LORD TENNYSON

12:57 p.m. I rush to the lunchroom, grateful that Madame's umbrella is keeping me dry as I go, so I can get food as quickly as possible. I shake off the umbrella and leave it just outside the lunchroom door.

The lunch volunteers can only give out one pizza slice at a time, to cut down on food waste. I'm happy that they give me a big one. There's also a spinach salad and roasted carrots. I scoop some onto my tray and hurry to my usual table. Abby, Sophy, Sadie, and I always sit together. Aisha, Ellie, and Lily sometimes join us, too. No one is at our table yet. I wonder for a second if Abby is going to sit somewhere else today. We haven't ever sat apart, unless one of us is out of school. I'm too hungry to think about it.

Sloane, of course, doesn't sit with us. She sits with Madison and Lucy and whoever else she thinks is worthy that week.

But today I notice her staring at me from two tables away. She has the same look on her face that she did in homeroom, when I raised my hand to tell Mr. Tripp what she'd said.

Right now, I couldn't care less about Sloane. I just want my lunch. I'm the first one at my table, but I cannot wait to start eating. I put my tray down, stow my backpack under the table, pick up the pizza, and take a bite.

12:58 p.m. The flavors of cheese and tomato and basil and slightly salty crust explode in my mouth. I'm not sure anything has ever tasted so good.

I feel a rush of gratitude for my meal. I guess that's one good thing about not eating breakfast. It makes you extra appreciative when lunchtime rolls around. (Okay, yes, it's better to have breakfast, too.) I keep eating, and my first slice of pizza is gone in about eight seconds.

I hear Sloane say to Lucy, not at all quietly, "God, it's like she hasn't eaten in a week." Obviously she's talking about me. But why? Why is she watching me eat? Why does she even care?

I'm ready for another slice of pizza. Even though the lunch volunteers only let us take one slice at a time, we're allowed to go back for more as many times as we'd like.

For a moment, Sloane's sneer keeps me glued to my seat. I don't want her making more comments about how long it's been since I last ate. They hit a little too close to the mark.

But my hunger wins out over my pride. Which is a good thing, because I am *hungry*, and it would be ridiculous to let my worries about Sloane keep me from eating. Plus, I have no idea what my dinner situation will be tonight. Or what I'll get to eat this weekend.

I need lunch.

So I ignore Sloane, grab my tray, and hurry back to the pizza line.

1:00 p.m. By this time, the line for pizza has grown longer, and I have to wait for a minute or two before I get my next slice. It lands on my tray, hot and cheesy, and I breathe in the smell. Yup, pizza smells good.

I head back to my table and see that Abby, Sophy, and Sadie have arrived. I relax. My friends feel kind of like a coat of armor. I don't feel as vulnerable to Sloane when they're around. And I'm especially glad to see Abby. She doesn't look up at me when I get to the table, or say hi to me, but at least she's there.

I plop my tray down, say hi to everyone, and sit. Suddenly I realize that I was in such a rush to get seconds that I forgot to wear my backpack to the lunch line. Instinctively, I reach my hand under the table to check on it.

I don't feel it. Maybe someone accidentally kicked it over when she sat down. I lean over and peek under the table so I can find it and pull it back close to me.

But it's not there.

I look again, as my ears start ringing and everything gets blurry and a feeling of panic rises up in my chest.

It's not anywhere. *No, no, no.* My backpack, packed with pretty much everything I own in the world, is gone.

1:01 p.m. Abby notices right away that I'm freaking out for real. And it seems like any mad feelings she had disappear instantly.

"Maya?" she says. "What's going on?"

I can barely speak. "My—my—my backpack," I splutter. "It's not here."

"Are you sure you brought it to lunch?" Sophy asks. "Maybe it's in your locker."

Abby, who doesn't know exactly why my backpack is so important to me these days but knows me well enough to notice that I've been carrying it everywhere, says to Sophy, "Yes, she brought it to lunch.

"Where did you put it?" Abby asks. "Did you leave it here when you went to get your food?"

I open my mouth to speak, but no sound comes out. I take a deep breath, fighting back the panic.

"It was under the table," I say. "I got my lunch first, and then I put it under there. But then . . ."

I take another breath. Abby waits and listens. She doesn't interrupt me like most people would at this point.

"I was really hungry and I went to get another slice of pizza. I didn't bring my backpack. The line was kind of long but I was only gone for two minutes. And when I got back, you all were here, but my backpack was gone."

"Okay," Abby says. "So we got here pretty soon after you got up. Your backpack has to be around here somewhere."

We both look around the lunchroom.

My eyes land on the table where Sloane was sitting just a few minutes ago. And that's when I notice. My backpack isn't all that has disappeared.

So has Sloane.

* * *

1:02 p.m. "Sloane," I say to Abby. "Sloane took it. She must have. She was just sitting at that table and now she's gone." I point toward her seat. There's a half-full glass of water still there. Lucy is still at the table, talking to Madison, who has joined her. But I don't see Sloane anywhere. "I know exactly where she was sitting, because she was making fun of how fast I ate my pizza, and she made sure I could hear her," I explain. "I know she took it."

I look around frantically. I want to run after Sloane, but I have no idea where she went.

"Maybe she did take it, or maybe she's just up getting food," Abby says.

"Hey, Lucy, where did Sloane go?" she calls out.

Lucy and Madison look up, surprised. The girls at our table don't usually talk to the girls at their table. They look around. "No idea," Madison says. Lucy shrugs and doesn't say anything.

"Let's go check the food line," Abby says.

"We need to hurry," I say.

Abby, Sophy, Sadie, and I take off at a run toward the food line. Immediately we hear Ms. Swanson, a sixth-grade teacher, call out, "Girls! No running."

We slow to a walk. Sophy glances at Ms. Swanson and says to me, "You should tell a teacher about your backpack."

"I know. I will. But I just want to look and see if Sloane is still in here." The panic bubbles up again. "I don't want anyone opening it. I don't want Sloane opening it. I can't . . ."

My throat feels like it's closing. I can't finish the thought. We're in the food service area now, and Sloane is nowhere to be seen.

I don't know what to do next. Luckily, Abby does. She can see I'm about to lose it, and she takes over. "Maya, you go tell a teacher right away. Sophy and Sadie, stay at our table in case Sloane comes back. I'll keep looking for your backpack. And Sloane."

Sophy and Sadie go back to our table, looking around as they go, and Abby takes off, jog-walking as fast as she can. I have a flash of gratitude for their help. For the fact that although I'm panicked, I'm not alone.

I take a deep breath and walk quickly to Ms. Swanson, the closest teacher to me. She's chatting with one of the parent lunch volunteers, but when she sees my face, she reluctantly trails off.

"Is everything okay? You're Maya, right?"

"Yes, I'm Maya," I say. "But no, everything is not okay. My backpack is gone," I explain.

"What do you mean?" she asks, confused. "Where did it go?"

I take another deep breath and try to explain it slowly

enough that she'll understand the first time. When fifth graders speak quickly, other fifth graders understand. Grown-ups, for some reason, usually don't.

"I brought my backpack to lunch. I usually wear it everywhere, but I left it under my lunch table for about a minute while I went to get food. When I got back, it was gone."

I can tell Ms. Swanson doesn't think this is urgent. She glances around the lunchroom. "Oh, I'm sure it's here somewhere," she says.

"It's not," I say firmly. "It's gone, and I'm almost positive I know who took it."

"Ohhhh, let's not jump to any conclusions," she says slowly and with a little singsong lilt to her voice. I can tell she doesn't feel like dealing with this. "Now, why don't you take another look around. Check under *all* the tables. If you don't find it, let me know." She turns back to her conversation.

"But it's not . . ." I'm about to argue with her, but I stop. I realize there's no point, and I see a better teacher option. My art teacher, Ms. Sherman, is across the lunchroom, heading toward the vegan entree area. I take off at a run toward her.

"Maya . . . no running!" Ms. Swanson reminds me, still using the singsong voice that only makes my panic worse, but I know she's ready to turn back to her adult conversation and won't be keeping an eye on me.

"Ms. Sherman!" I shout, just as she's about to get a bowl of soup. She turns to look, sees me—and what must be an almost insanely frantic look on my face— and immediately returns the ladle to the soup tureen.

"Maya! What happened?" She has the right level of urgency in her voice. She gets that something is up. Something real. She won't brush me off so she can get back to gossiping with another grown-up.

"Ms. Sherman," I say breathlessly, and get straight to the point. "Someone took my backpack."

She doesn't question that fact. She gets right down to business. "Oh man. Okay. We are going to find it," she says. "Where was it?"

I explain about leaving it under the table in the lunchroom when going back for seconds. "I know I shouldn't have done that, but that was the only time all day I didn't have it right with me. I was just so hungry!" Tears well up again.

"Hey, Maya," she says. "You should be able to leave your backpack anywhere you want to at this school and not have to worry about it being taken. This is not your fault."

"Okay," I say, brushing away a tear that's about to tumble onto my cheek.

"How long ago did this happen?" she asks.

"Maybe . . . I don't know. Five minutes ago," I say.

"It can't have gone far, then," she says. She glances

around, then lowers her voice. "Do you have any idea who might have taken it?"

I nod. "I think it was Sloane," I say quietly. "Actually, I'm almost positive."

She doesn't ask me why I think that. She also doesn't look surprised.

Abby rushes back in right then, out of breath. "I looked everywhere I could think of," she says. "But I didn't find it. And . . . um . . . and . . ." She glances uncomfortably at Ms. Sherman.

"What else?" Ms. Sherman asks.

"Well, I didn't see Sloane anywhere, either," Abby says in a rush.

"You're sure she's not in the lunchroom?" Ms. Sherman asks.

"She's gone," I say. "She was here, at a table right near mine. But she's not here anymore."

"Come with me," Ms. Sherman says. "Let's see what we can find." She abandons her tray and guides Abby and me out of the lunchroom.

1:06 p.m. On days when it's not raining, seventh and eighth graders are allowed to eat outside if they want to, at the tables in the courtyard outside the lunchroom or on the wide steps that lead to the school library. But today the courtyard, tables, and steps are all empty, slick with rain. Raindrops are pounding the hard surfaces and splashing into growing puddles. But it seems eerily silent to me as I scan the area and don't see anyone or anything.

I'm not sure what I was expecting to find right outside the lunchroom, but my heart sinks again at the emptiness.

Ms. Sherman quickly breaks the silence. "Nothing to see here, girls. Let's get going." She's not wearing a raincoat or anything, but she dashes across the courtyard to the library entrance. It's connected to the covered walkway that leads to the upper-school lockers and classrooms. Abby and I follow her.

"Library first," Ms. Sherman says. That makes sense. Our lunch period goes until 1:25, but if we finish early, fifth and sixth graders can go outside with the older girls (when it's not raining) or go to the library. Not surprisingly, I take the library option fairly often myself. I've never once seen Sloane in there, but there's a first time for everything. And it's the only place other than the lunchroom where she's technically allowed to be right now.

1:07 p.m. The library is quiet when we enter. One eighth grader, Amelia, has braved the rain to cross from the lunchroom to the library. She's shaking the water droplets off her raincoat. She glances toward us when we open the door but loses interest immediately when she sees it's two fifth graders and a teacher. She says a quick "Hi, Ms. Sherman."

"Hi, Amelia," Ms. Sherman says. "Has anyone else come in here from lunch?"

"Don't think so," Amelia replies with a shrug, and starts heading toward the YA section.

"Can you let us know if you see anyone back there?" I call out.

She looks back at me, a little surprised. "Um, sure?" she says, and keeps walking. We don't hear from her again.

We peek into the lower-school area and down some of the aisles of books but don't see or hear anything.

"Let's move on," Ms. Sherman says.

From the library, we hurry down the covered walkway, peeking into all the classrooms. We don't find anything or see anyone. We reach the end of the walkway, where the stairs lead to more classrooms and the fifth- and sixth-grade lockers.

We're about to climb the stairs when we hear someone hurrying down them, breathing heavily. The person turns the corner of the stairs and comes into view.

And there she is.

It's Sloane.

* * *

1:10 p.m. At the sight of Sloane, I feel the heat of anger coursing through me. As much as I usually try to contain myself around her, I can't right now.

"Where is it?" I demand. I wish I sounded calm and cool and in charge, but it comes out somewhere between a squeak and a scream.

She stares at me with wide eyes, cocks her head to one side, and smirks. "I have no idea *what* you're talking about."

"You know exactly what she's talking about," Abby says. She sounds calm, cool, and in charge. "Where. Is. It?"

I can tell Sloane wants to say something extra nasty, but Ms. Sherman is there, so she doesn't.

Instead she kind of flutters her eyelashes, all innocence and sweetness, and says in a syrupy voice, "I really don't know what you're talking about. Ms. Sherman, can I go now?"

As she's saying it, though, I swear I see her eyes darting to the side. In mystery books that's always a giveaway that someone is lying. But I can't exactly prove anything by saying, *Did you see? Her eyes moved!*

Ms. Sherman peers at Sloane and says, "You can go in a moment, Sloane. But first, can you please tell me what you're doing here? You should be at lunch or in the library."

"Oh, Ms. Sherman, I *was* in the library . . . but . . . I thought I had . . . a book to return," Sloane says sweetly. "So I came up to my locker to grab it."

"Uh-huh," Ms. Sherman says. "And where is the book?"

"The book?" Sloane says. "Oh! I . . . I . . . had already returned it." Her eyes are darting like crazy now. But again, that's not exactly something I could use as evidence.

"Oh, great," says Ms. Sherman. Did I hear a hint of sarcasm in her voice? Yes, I think I did. She knows Sloane's not telling the truth.

"And you're certain you didn't take anything belonging to Maya?" Ms. Sherman asks.

"Of course not!" Sloane exclaims. "What would *I* want with her backpack, anyway?"

Ms. Sherman pauses, gazing steadily at Sloane.

Sloane shifts uncomfortably. "Um, can I go now?" she asks.

"Sloane," Ms. Sherman says quietly, "how did you know we were talking about Maya's backpack?"

1:14 p.m. The look of terror that appears on Sloane's face, just for an instant, tells me she knows she's caught.

But she regains composure quickly. And gets nasty, too. If we weren't talking about something she stole from me, I'd be kind of impressed by her recovery. "Well, what *else* could she be looking for? It's not like she has anything besides that backpack." She practically spits the last word. And then she adds, "Anyway, why don't you ask *her?*" She points at Abby.

"Now that I think about it, I'm pretty sure *she* had Maya's backpack before lunch. I guess that's why I was thinking about the backpack. Because I saw *her* with it," Sloane says, pointing again, "and it's just weird to see it anywhere but right with Maya, all the time."

Abby's eyes widen. "I did *not* take Maya's backpack."

"I don't know, Maya," Sloane says in a voice full of fake concern. "Maybe you should look for your backpack in Abby's locker. That's all I'm saying."

"That's enough, Sloane," Ms. Sherman says. "Right now I need you to go straight to Ms. Thompson's office."

Getting sent to the school head's office is serious. I can't believe Sloane is finally, maybe, actually going to face consequences for something she did.

"What?" Sloane sputters. "I have to go to humanities soon."

"No," Ms. Sherman says quietly. "You *have* to go to Ms. Thompson's office. I'll let your humanities teacher know. And please tell Ms. Thompson's assistant that I will be meeting you there in ten minutes."

Sloane narrows her eyes at Abby and me, then turns in a huff and does what she's told.

1:18 p.m. My legs feel like they have weights attached to them as Abby, Ms. Sherman, and I climb the stairs to the second floor. When we get there, Ms. Sherman says, "Maya, why don't you check your locker, just in case? And, well . . . might as well check Abby's locker, too." She opens the door to the fifth-grade humanities classroom to do a quick search.

"But, Ms. Sherman," Abby protests, "I didn't—"

"I know you didn't," Ms. Sherman says. "But maybe someone else did."

"Okay," I say. "But it's definitely not in my locker. At least," I say, with a sense of foreboding, "I didn't leave it there."

The word "lockers" isn't exactly accurate to describe the spots where we keep our stuff—because although they look like traditional lockers, no one uses locks. It's part of the school honor code. No one is allowed to open anyone else's locker without permission, so why would we need locks? (And, the faculty has told us, fiddling with locks would just slow us down, and they don't need to give us another excuse for being late to class.) So, no locks.

Which is fine, most of the time. Unless someone like Sloane decides she's going to mess with another student.

I open my locker.

Nothing.

Then I open Abby's, which is right next to mine.

And there's my backpack.

1:20 p.m. My backpack is dripping wet. Not just caught-in-the-rain-for-a-minute wet, but intentionally soaked wet.

Abby, right by my side, stares at it.

"Maya," she says. "I didn't . . . I would never. How did that . . . ?"

"Sloane," I say. "That's how. I know you didn't."

Because despite the fact that she got mad at me, and even though I haven't been able to bring myself to tell her about living in the shelter, I know I can trust Abby completely.

That's a good feeling.

Abby gingerly reaches into her locker and pulls out the backpack. The stuff on the bottom of her locker is all wet, too.

"We found it," I call to Ms. Sherman. "In Abby's

locker. But I did *not* leave it here. And neither did Abby."

She emerges from the classroom and sees Abby holding the dripping backpack.

"No, that doesn't look like something that's been left in a locker for very long," Ms. Sherman says. She sighs. "I'm glad you found it, though. Let's see if everything is still intact."

I stare at the backpack. I'm afraid to look inside. I'm terrified that something will be gone.

I'm right.

1:22 p.m. When I take the backpack from Abby, right away I can tell something is wrong. It's way too light. The main compartment is already unzipped. I peer inside.

It's empty.

My books. My favorite books. The only ones I kept when we left our house. And the stuffed dog I've had since I was a baby. My sketchbook. My colored pencils.

They're gone.

My money. $17.32. All the money I had in the world.

It's gone, too.

But that's not all.

My photo of my family—Mama, Daddy, Gabby, and me—was tucked inside my copy of *Charlie and the*

Chocolate Factory. The note from my dad was also in the backpack. Which means they're gone, too.

My head hurts. My heart hurts. My legs feel weak.

I lean back against one of the closed lockers, then slide down and slump onto the floor. I let go of the backpack and put my head down on my bent knees.

"It's gone," I say.

"What's gone?" Abby asks gently as she sits next to me on the floor.

"Everything."

9

ReADiNG TiMe

I'm so thankful for friendship.

—*LUCY MAUD MONTGOMERY*

1:23 p.m. Abby puts her hand on my back. She doesn't say anything. Ms. Sherman, who is now sitting next to me, is quiet, too. Finally I pick my head up.

"At least I already turned in my homework folder," I say.

"But . . . what else was in there, Maya?" Abby asks.

"Promise you won't laugh," I say.

"Maya," Abby says. "Why would we laugh? Nothing about this is funny."

"Okay," I say. "Well, I had a bunch of my favorite books. The ones I love to read over and over again. And Gilbert," I say. Abby knows the name of my favorite stuffed animal. "And my favorite picture of my whole family, and all my money in a ziplock bag, and the last note my dad wrote me before his accident."

Abby stares at me.

"So that's why you never want to leave your backpack anywhere," she says. "Maya, I'm so sorry. But . . ." She trails off. I know she wants to ask me *why* I'm carrying all that stuff around with me, everywhere and every day.

She doesn't, though.

"Well, we know who took the backpack. I'm going to deal with her now—and find out what happened to everything inside," Ms. Sherman says. She touches my arm. "I'm so, so sorry, Maya. But this isn't finished."

Ms. Sherman glances at her watch. "Lunch is over in—well, it's over now," she says as the bell rings. Which means a stampede of girls is coming soon.

I can't deal with having a bunch of people asking me why I'm sitting on the floor. So even though I feel like a bag of rocks, I heave myself up to standing. Abby stands, too.

"Maya, do you want to take a break?" Ms. Sherman asks.

I consider this. I have a long humanities period right now, and since it's a Friday, the chances are good that we'll get a long free reading period. I can handle that. I *need* that. Plus, Abby's in my humanities class. And I'm pretty sure Sloane won't be. Not today.

"That's all right, Ms. Sherman," I say. "I can go to humanities."

"I'll be with her," Abby says.

"Okay," says Ms. Sherman. "But if you change your mind, take a break. Talk to Ms. Choi. Tell her I told you a break is a good idea, and that I can explain," she says with a smile. Ms. Choi is another one of my favorite teachers, and Ms. Sherman and Ms. Choi are good friends.

"Sounds good," I say, smiling back weakly.

"And come find me during conference time," Ms. Sherman adds. Conference time is a fifteen-minute block in our homerooms before our closing meeting, when we can work on homework or study for quizzes or go to teachers for extra help. "I'll let you know if anything turns up."

"Thanks, Ms. Sherman," I say. Despite everything, I have another moment of feeling grateful. This time for my teacher.

"No need to thank me, Maya," Ms. Sherman says. "I'm here for you. And I'll see you during conference." She smiles again and heads off to see Sloane.

I breathe in deeply, gearing up to walk to our humanities classroom. It's about twenty-five feet away, but it feels far right now.

* * *

1:26 p.m. Before I take a step, Abby reaches for my backpack. And shakes it a little. "Wait a second. Are you sure *everything* is gone? Have you checked all the pockets and stuff?"

A flicker of hope lights in my chest.

The books are definitely gone. So are my art supplies. But.

I unzip a small pocket at the back of the main compartment. I think I might have . . . yes. I pull out Gilbert. Of course. That's where I always keep him during school.

I feel around the pocket more, and I'm shocked to realize that my money bag is there as well. That's right. I moved it back there so it would be more hidden, too.

And finally, I reach one finger into the smallest zippered compartment at the very back of the bag. I hold my breath, then slowly exhale.

It's there.

The note from my dad, folded tightly into a tiny square.

I still have it.

1:27 p.m. Relief floods my entire body. The books, I guess, are replaceable. So are the art supplies. Even the photo is replaceable. The money would have been replaceable, too, maybe, somehow, sometime. Although

I'm glad I still have it. But the note feels like the strongest link I have to my dad. As long as I have it, I feel like he's still with me—and like he might even get better.

And then the tears that have been threatening all day come flooding out. This time, I don't even try to stop them.

Abby doesn't try to get me to stop crying, either. She just lets me sob, my forehead against the door of my locker. She puts her hand on my back and says nothing. But she's with me. That's exactly what I need. Someone telling you to stop crying when you need to cry is the worst.

What sounds like a thousand girls come streaming into the hallway. I don't look up. Although I can sense people slowing down and staring when they see me crying, no one says anything. I'm guessing Abby is giving them one of her "stay away" looks.

My tears keep flowing as the commotion around me swells and then subsides.

The tears slow, and then stop, and I look up.

"Thanks, Abby," I say.

"For what?" she asks.

For being my friend even though I'm not telling you the whole truth, I think. *For being a good, kind person. For helping me find my backpack. For letting me cry. For being someone who wouldn't let the fact that I'm living in a shelter change the way you think about me.* I think all of those things, and I'm still planning to tell her, but right at this moment I'm too tired to say the words. I will, though. I will tell her everything. But for now, I simply say, "Just . . . for everything."

She smiles at me, and I know she understands.

1:30 p.m. We have an hour-long humanities period today, and it's as if Ms. Choi knows some of us are wiped out by the day and the week (not to mention the whole last month). She tells us we're going to have a free reading period, for most of the class, with some reflecting and journaling time at the end. This I can handle.

She says we can choose any book we want from the middle shelf. I can't believe my luck, but there's a copy of *Anne of Green Gables* there. So I get to spend the next hour reading and writing about one of my favorite books. One of the books I just lost. I fight back tears when I think about that. I'm tired of wanting to cry.

I open the book and start at the beginning. "Mrs. Rachel Lynde lived just where the Avonlea main road dipped down into a little hollow, fringed with alders and ladies' eardrops. . . ." And I am lost in the world of Avonlea.

Anne Shirley had it worse than I did, before the Cuthberts adopted her from the orphanage. That's what I write about in my journal—how positive and optimistic and grateful Anne was, no matter how difficult things were, and whether that's even realistic, as much as I love reading about it. It's hard to be positive all the time. Because some days are really tough.

But some days get better.

10

TRuTH TiMe

Truth lifts the heart.

—RUMI

2:30 p.m. Our reading and journaling time flies by, and when it's over, Abby and I leave the humanities room together and head to the art room.

On the way there, I know it's time to tell her. I stop walking. Abby gets a few steps ahead of me, notices I'm not with her, and turns back to me. "Maya . . . ?"

I take a deep breath. "I have to tell you something," I say.

"What is it?" she asks, and waits, looking at me with her kind eyes.

It will be okay.

"I really do want to have a sleepover," I blurt out.

She can tell I'm not done. She half smiles and waits for me to go on.

"But I feel weird about leaving Mama and Gabby right now. And you can't come to my house," I say. "Because we don't have a house."

Abby looks confused, but she lets me finish.

"When we moved out of our house, we didn't move to . . . we couldn't . . ."

My face is flushed, and my cheeks are wet. I choke back a sob.

"We moved to a homeless shelter."

2:32 p.m. Abby doesn't say anything. She just comes over and hugs me, and lets me cry and cry, for the second time today.

When I stop crying, I pull away to look at her. She's crying, too.

"Maya, I didn't . . . I didn't know. I'm so sorry I kept bugging you about a sleepover."

I half laugh. "That's okay."

"But why didn't you tell me? Why didn't you come stay with us? Why . . . I'm sorry."

I breathe in deeply and let it out.

"I don't know why," I say. "I haven't told anyone. I was embarrassed or something. It's a hard thing to tell.

And at school I wanted it to feel like everything was normal."

"You can tell me anything," she says. "You don't ever have to be embarrassed."

"I know," I say. And I do.

"I will tell you all about it," I promise. "But we should go to see Ms. Sherman now. She'll wonder where we are."

"Tell me whenever you're ready," Abby says. "And come for a sleepover whenever you're ready, too."

I smile and wipe the last of my tears away. She wipes away her tears and hugs me again, and then we make our way to the art studio.

2:37 p.m. Ms. Sherman is in there, cleaning up the pottery wheels and putting clay away. She stops when she hears us come in.

"Hi, girls," she says. "You okay, Maya?"

"I'm okay," I say. "And you know what? Not everything was gone from my backpack. There were a couple of things that I had zipped into little pockets inside. They were still there."

"Hey, that's great," Ms. Sherman says. "But it doesn't change the fact that this should *not* have happened. And just so you know, Sloane is spending the rest of the day in Ms. Thompson's office—and then she is not invited back to school until after winter break. And she'll have a whole bunch of makeup work to do over the break."

"She got suspended?" I ask, shocked. I can't think of a time when Sloane has even been caught doing something mean—which is kind of amazing, given how often it happens—and I certainly can't remember her ever, ever facing consequences for something.

"Of course she did. She stole. She lied. She went into Abby's locker without permission. She violated the honor code," Ms. Sherman says. "Quite frankly, I could have had her expelled."

"You mean she admitted it?" I ask, even more shocked.

"Nope," Ms. Sherman says. "She never did, outright. But she gave herself away so many times that it was a little ridiculous. And," she adds, to my astonishment, "someone saw her do it, and reported it."

"What?" I say. "Someone told on Sloane? Who?"

"I promised I wouldn't say," Ms. Sherman says. "But there are people on your side out there."

I wonder if it was Lucy. Whoever it was, I'm grateful.

And then, for a moment, I'm hopeful. "Did you find out what she did with my stuff? Can I get it back?"

Ms. Sherman shakes her head sadly. "Apparently she unzipped it and dumped everything—well, I guess not *everything*, right?—into the big garbage compactor in the kitchen. Whatever was in your bag is smushed under a day's worth of lunch waste. And then she drenched the bag in a puddle. Lovely."

I feel deflated again.

"Oh," I say.

And then something occurs to me.

"Her parents are going to be really mad at you," I say. "They give a lot of money to this school, and everyone knows it. And I've always thought that might be one of the reasons she never gets in trouble." And then I groan. "And she's going to be worse than ever to me."

"First of all, let me worry about her parents," Ms. Sherman says. "And second of all, no, she isn't."

"Yes, she is," I insist.

"Maya, Ms. Thompson told her that if she ever pulls any kind of stunt like this again, on you or anyone, she will be expelled. And Sloane knew she was serious."

I roll my eyes. "She'll find a way. She always does."

"Maybe," Ms. Sherman says. "But if she does, you can tell me about it. Or Ms. Thompson. Right away. And you, Maya, can get through it."

"You can tell me, too," Abby says. "And you know I'll always be on your side."

I know she will. She was today, even when she was mad at me. I pause, considering.

"What are you thinking about?" Ms. Sherman asks.

"I'm thinking about why," I say. "Why? *Why* does she do stuff like this? To me? To everyone?"

Ms. Sherman looks at me and says, as if it's obvious, "I think Sloane targets you because she's jealous."

2:40 p.m. *"Jealous?"* I say incredulously. "What are you even talking about? She has everything. I have . . ." I trail off and look at my dripping backpack.

"You have what she doesn't," Ms. Sherman says gently. "The most important thing."

"An empty, wet backpack? Believe me, she doesn't want a backpack. She only wants a messenger bag. Or, you know, ten messenger bags in ten different colors."

Abby half snorts, half giggles.

"Well, that may be true," Ms. Sherman says. "But it wasn't about the bag itself. What do you care about most in that bag?" she asks.

"The note and the . . . oh. The stuff from my family," I say, with a flicker of understanding.

"Right," says Ms. Sherman. "Your family matters to you more than any *things* ever could. I know your family is in crisis right now—I don't think Sloane understands that—but through it all, you have a little sister who adores you and a mom who loves you more than anything in the world. And," she adds, with a smile at Abby, "you have good, true friends."

Even though Ms. Sherman doesn't know the full extent of my family crisis, she's right about how much we love each other. Even on our very worst days, I always know that.

"Sloane has a family, too," I say. And suddenly I'm angry again. "And it's ridiculous to say that because my family loves me, it's okay for her to do what she does to me. And to everyone. She's awful."

"Believe me, Maya, I am not saying it's okay. That's why she's been suspended," Ms. Sherman says. "But just remember that everyone, even the one who is worst to us, is fighting her own battles. Sloane's family, despite what things look like from the outside, is a mess on the inside. I can't say anything more than that, but she has never had anything close to the love and support you have."

I think about Sloane's enormous house—make that two houses—and all her stuff, and her three rooms, and the way her mother couldn't wait to get away from us during our one and only play date, and how I've heard that her father moved out years ago and she hasn't seen him since, and that her mother leaves for months at a time while Sloane stays with a team of nannies.

And I realize that, enormous house or no enormous house, I wouldn't trade places with her for anything.

* * *

2:43 p.m. Abby and I leave the art room and race toward our homerooms so we won't be late for our closing meetings. If our homerooms are dismissed at slightly different times, I might not see her again until Monday.

"Thanks, Abby," I say again.

"You don't have to thank me," she says. "But let's just do something together soon. Anything. It doesn't have to be a sleepover. I miss you."

"Yes," I say. "I miss you, too."

Abby and I have to head in different directions now. She ducks into her homeroom. I still have to cross a courtyard. I'm going to get soaked, again. Suddenly I remember Madame's umbrella. I still need to return it, but I don't have it. I run to the lunchroom and am relieved to find it's still where I left it, leaning against the wall near the doorway. I grab it and race to the French classroom. Madame isn't there, but the door is unlocked and the lights are still on. I hurry in to leave it by her desk, still grateful that it kept me dry for part of today—and that she was so willing to share it. I pause for a second to soak up the cozy feeling this room always gives me, then sprint to my homeroom.

2:46 p.m. I am wet, wiped out, and one minute late for closing meeting, but Mr. Tripp hasn't started yet—and Sloane isn't there to point it out.

I'm even more relieved she's not there when Mr. Tripp reminds us about our visit to the food pantry next week, and the food drive. It occurs to me that because I still have my money, I'll be able to buy a can for the food drive. That's one more thing I'm grateful Sloane didn't steal.

Mr. Tripp tells us an email will be going out about it and that our parents can sign the permission slip online. Then he adds, "Over the weekend, I'd like you to spend some time thinking about what it really means to be homeless—and what some of the deeper implications of food insecurity might be."

Well, I will be thinking about all of that. I can't get away from it. There's plenty I could share about being homeless—how exhausting it is, how humiliating it feels, and how many truly good people with painful stories are homeless.

Maybe I will, someday. But that feels too hard. For now, just getting through the day in fifth grade is hard enough.

11

DiSMiSSAL TiMe

This is one moment,
But know that another
Shall pierce you with a sudden painful joy

—*T. S. ELIOT*

2:54 p.m. "Get out of here, girls," says Mr. Tripp. "Those of you who turned in your homework folders this morning can grab them on the way out. Have a great weekend."

Everyone except me starts chattering excitedly. I get it. Friday afternoon used to be one of my favorite times of the week. No matter how much you like school, it's a good feeling to be set free and have the whole weekend ahead of you.

But when I know I'll be spending the whole weekend either at our shelter or at the hospital, it doesn't feel so exciting.

* * *

2:55 p.m. There's a crowd of girls heading toward the school's main entrance. I pull over to the side of the courtyard to let them by, and peek into my homework folder. On the top page is a writing assignment with a big smiley face from Ms. Choi and *Beautiful work, Maya!* written in red pencil. It gives me a quick boost of energy. I'll save the rest of the comments for the weekend.

School doesn't officially get out until three o'clock. But our teachers usually let us out a few minutes before that, so we're ready to be picked up or get to our after-school activities right on time. Last fall, before my dad's accident, I usually stayed after school. I was on the cross-country team, and I had practice or a race three or four days a week. And my dad came to almost every race to cheer for my team and me.

I'm glad I don't have cross-country practice today. Even after reading Ms. Choi's comment, I don't have anything close to enough energy for that.

I hope I'm not this tired all the time next fall. I want to be on the team again.

And I really hope my dad can come to my races.

2:57 p.m. I make my way to the entrance, and although no one is coming to get me today and I can leave whenever I want, I stay under the awning with the girls who are waiting for rides. I clutch my backpack straps tightly. I won't be letting this backpack out of my sight again anytime soon. Even though it's still damp from whatever puddle Sloane dunked it in, it feels like a security blanket on my back.

Which is exactly what I need right now.

Well, that and an umbrella.

The rain has lightened up a bit, but it's still coming down, and I'm not looking forward to the journey home. This day has drained me. I feel like I've run the longest cross-country race of my life.

The idea of walking three blocks in the rain to the bus stop, riding the bus, changing buses by myself, and getting off the bus in the neighborhood of my shelter when it's starting to get dark . . . it's all daunting. I'm not sure I can do it.

How I wish I'd said yes to a sleepover *tonight* with Abby, and gotten a ride to her house in a warm car. Or that I could just walk to my old house and have pizza for dinner. Or at least that Mama and Gabby could be with me on the bus.

I close my eyes and hike up my shoulders as I brace myself for getting drenched on the way to the bus stop.

When I open my eyes, I see someone coming up the walkway toward my school, holding a little girl's hand and carrying a huge umbrella.

I blink and look again.

It can't be. We don't have an umbrella like that.

But it is.

Mama and Gabby are here.

2:59 p.m. I can't believe it. They're here. With an umbrella. My shoulders relax, and I loosen the iron grip I had on my backpack straps. It's still cold outside, but I feel a rush of warmth coming from inside me.

I blink back tears—again—but this time I think they're mostly happy tears. I can't tell which emotion is which right now. That's how it is when you're overwhelmed. All day I've felt like I've been carrying loads of bricks up a steep hill and have been constantly about to fall.

And it's as if someone just started propping me up and carrying half the bricks.

When they get closer, I notice that Mama is smiling. It's a big, real smile. The biggest and realest I've seen on her in months. Only when I see that smile do I realize how absent it has been.

And how much I've missed it.

3:00 p.m. When Mama and Gabby reach the steps under the awning, Mama shakes the umbrella off over the steps, puts it down upside down, and—still holding Gabby's hand with one hand—pulls me in to her with the other. "My Maya," she says.

"My Mama," I say, my voice muffled as I lean against her shoulder.

We stand like that, without saying anything else, for a few seconds. Until Gabby starts pulling at my hand. "I want my Maya!" she cries. So I lean down and scoop her up in a big bear hug. A gust of wind almost sweeps the umbrella away, but Mama yanks it back just in time.

"Oops!" she says. "This thing is so big, it could hurt someone."

As Gabby nuzzles into my neck, I say, "About that thing—where did you get the umbrella?"

Just then Sloane's huge black SUV pulls up to the front steps. They have a driver, and he's driving. I wonder if Sloane's mother is in there, but I can't see through the dark windows. I wonder for a second if Sloane will be in trouble for getting suspended, but I doubt that.

"Let's start walking," Mama says, glancing at the monstrous car. She doesn't know what happened today, but she does know Sloane isn't my favorite. "I'll tell you as we go."

3:01 p.m. Mama struggles to keep the umbrella upright in the wind with one hand. "Maya, could you hold

Gabby's hand, please? That will make it easier for me to keep us all dry."

Gabby slips her hand into mine, then pulls my hand toward her face and gives it a quick kiss.

"I wuv my Maya," she says.

"I love you, too, Gabby girl," I say.

12

HoPe TiMe

Love comforteth like sunshine after rain.

—WILLIAM SHAKESPEARE

3:02 p.m. "Thanks for coming, Mama," I say. "You too, Gabby girl."

"I'm so glad we could, my Maya," Mama says, then stops to look at me. "And I have something to tell you."

"Something about the job?" I ask.

"Make that two somethings," she says. "But the first is about your dad."

I feel goose bumps rise all over my skin. I can't believe I didn't ask about him first. But for months, there's been no news, or only bad news, and I've gotten used to it. And it occurs to me that this could be more bad news.

Except . . . Mama's still smiling.

"Did something happen?" I ask.

"Something happened," she says. "You know they put the breathing tube through his neck and they've been waiting for him to be awake enough so they could try today to take him off the ventilator. Well, today he was awake enough. He was awake, Maya! And it worked. Or rather, his lungs worked. He can breathe on his own."

For a moment I can't make a sound. I knew this *could* happen today, but I didn't know if it would. Finally I sputter, "He—he's awake? He can?" The chills are back, and my eyes fill up with tears. "But does that mean . . . is he all better?"

She puts her arm around me. "No, sweetie. Not yet. They have to give his lungs much more time to recover all the way. They don't know how long. And, Maya," she adds, "they still don't understand the extent of his brain injuries. That's what they'll be figuring out over the next few weeks. He might not have his memory, or he might not be able to speak, or . . . well, they just don't know yet. But this is good news."

"Oh," I say, feeling deflated after getting my hopes up.

"Would you like to go see him today?" Mama asks.

"Today?" I ask, surprised. "But aren't visiting hours almost over for today?" On weekdays, kids are only allowed to visit from two to four. Which I remember because they're the same visiting hours as in *Madeline,* one of my favorite picture books. But which means I can't visit my dad during the week. Karen, the head nurse on my dad's floor, doesn't let anyone start a visit after three-thirty.

"Sabrina is going to sneak us in today, just for a second." Sabrina is one of my dad's nurses, and she's really nice. "She wants you to be able to see him."

"Can I talk to him?" I ask, the goose bumps returning. "Can he talk to me?"

"You can, sweetie," Mama says. "I don't know how awake he will be when we get there, and he hasn't talked yet, but you can definitely talk to him."

"So nothing's different," I mutter.

"Maya," Mama says, looking into my eyes, "a lot is different. I promise you, this is the best news we've had in months. His lungs are working. He's able to wake up. I just didn't want you to think he was all better. I always want to be honest with you. Okay?"

"Okay," I say. "Thanks, Mama."

I know it's good news. But after today, I guess I'm hoping for even better news.

And then Mama gives me some.

3:06 p.m. We start walking again, toward the bus stop. "Mama, what's the other something you had to tell me?" I ask.

"Well," she says, "you know I had the job interview today."

As if I could have forgotten.

"Um, yeah, I think I remember something about that," I say. "How was it?"

"It was wonderful, actually. It's an amazing school, and it's a great fit for me. And," she says, "they have a spot for Gabby."

"Does that mean . . . ?" I'm almost afraid to ask what I want to ask.

Mama smiles and stops walking. I stop, too, and so does Gabby. Mama uses her free hand to pull me close to her again.

"Yes, Maya. The director offered me the job," Mama says. "And, yes, I accepted."

I realize I've been holding my breath, waiting to hear what Mama was going to say. I exhale, and my whole body relaxes.

"So . . . how . . . when do you . . . can we . . . ?" Questions jumble together in my brain, and I don't know what to ask first.

We keep standing where we are, under the umbrella, as Mama explains everything. She'll start working there right after winter break, and Gabby can start then, too.

Besides running the art program for the school, Mama will be in charge of preparing healthy snacks for everyone—all allergen-free—using organic ingredients from the school's kitchen and garden, and often involving the students. She and Gabby will be there from nine to two every day, so they'll be able to take me to school and pick me up on the bus.

"But can we . . . will we be able to . . . ?" I can't quite get the words out. But I want to know if we can move out of the shelter.

Mama knows what I'm asking.

"Not right away," Mama says. "The salary isn't very high. But there's something I didn't tell you yet. One of the founders of the school has a small cottage in her backyard."

My ears perk up. Backyard cottages are a thing in some places in San Francisco, even though the city lots aren't huge. Mama must be telling me about this for a reason. She goes on. "She rents it to new teachers from the school, for much less rent than just about anywhere in the city, usually for six months at a time, so teachers who need some support can save up and find a place."

"Could we . . . ?" I think I know what she's going to say, but it almost seems too good to be true.

Mama smiles again. "She usually rents it to teachers who've just graduated from college, so they have time to save money before they try to rent an apartment. But I explained our situation—"

"Mama!" I interrupt. "You told them?"

"It's all right, Maya," she says. "Really, it is. I thought they needed to understand what our family is going through. So, yes, I told them. And they're going to try help us. There's a teacher living in the cottage now, and they can't ask her to leave immediately. But they'll explain that something has come up and see if she's open to a different arrangement. It might take several months—or there's a slight chance we could move in at the beginning of next month. We'll know soon."

The beginning of next month. I latch on to that. That's one month from today. I don't want to get too excited, but even the idea, the possibility of having a home in one month, fills me with warmth and hope. The last month of living in a shelter has been the longest month I can remember. But maybe, possibly, knowing that it could end soon might make it a little easier to get through another month. Or however many more months we need to get through.

And then I realize something. "Mama!" I say again. "We *could* have a home again before my birthday!"

"Birfday!" Gabby cries. "My Maya, picky up!"

I lean down and scoop her into my arms.

"Maybe," Mama says. "Maybe. I hope so."

"I was thinking today about birthday wishes, and that was one of them," I say. "But I didn't think it could come true."

"Oh, my Maya," Mama says, and squeezes me tight. "There is a chance it could come true. And this might sound strange, given everything, but today . . . today I feel lucky."

Standing here, in the rain, snuggled against Mama, with Gabby snuggled against me, I feel the worst parts of this day and the last month and the last three months wash away. And I feel a little lucky, too.

3:11 p.m. "But, Mama," I say. "You still didn't explain about the umbrella."

"Oh, right!" she says. "Well, the rain started coming down while we were at the interview. And the head of the school noticed that we didn't have an umbrella or raincoats. So she gave this to us."

"She just . . . she just gave it to you? To keep?" I ask. It's a really nice, new umbrella. It feels like forever since we've had something nice and new.

"Well, I'm going to be working there. And they have an outdoor education program. All the classes spend a few hours each week exploring the Presidio"—that's the national park with lots of trails and forests, right in the middle of San Francisco—"and they go rain or shine. So all teachers get a school umbrella."

She points to the school logo, which I can make out pretty well, even from under the umbrella. It's an image of a tree, sheltering birds on its branches and people underneath. Kind of like the umbrella is sheltering us right now.

The image on the umbrella reminds me of something. "Mama," I say to her as we walk slowly, all trying to stay dry under the umbrella, "where do birds go when it rains?"

"Good question," she says. "Well, they don't mind a little drizzle, but when it starts raining hard, like it is now, they take shelter in whatever safe place they can find. Maybe in a tree, or maybe under the eaves of a house."

"Can they really stay dry in a tree?" I ask.

"They can, actually. Or as dry as they need to be to keep warm enough, anyway."

I look at the tree in the logo. It's not perfect. It's not a cozy birdhouse with a roof and a soft nest. But it's something.

"Good," I say. "I'm glad they have a place to go."

3:13 p.m. "Speaking of a place to go," Mama says. "Do you both want to go somewhere fun tomorrow?"

"You mean . . . we don't have to spend the whole day at . . ." I pause. I'm having trouble forming complete thoughts. I look around to make sure no one is close enough to hear me.

"We don't have to spend the whole day at the

shelter?" I whisper. "Even if it's raining? Inside places cost money."

Mama looks sad for a moment. "Oh, sweetie. You . . . Oh, you shouldn't have to be worried about this all the time. You're mostly right, but I've been thinking about it. There are places we can go, and I'm sorry I haven't been doing a good job of coming up with fun things. Let's see. We can go to the library anytime. And we still have our library cards. We can go to the botanical garden, if it stops raining. Or we can go to the Legion of Honor. It's free on Saturdays for anyone who lives in San Francisco."

I love this idea. But something worries me. "Do we count, Mama?"

Mama looks at me. "What do you mean?"

"I mean, do we count as living in San Francisco? Now that we don't really even have our own place to live? Isn't that just for the people with houses?"

"We count," Mama says firmly. "People with houses are not the only ones who count."

At this, I perk up. The Legion of Honor is an art museum near my school. It has one room that Mama and I especially love, full of art by Impressionist painters like Claude Monet and Pierre Renoir. Our favorite is an enormous Monet painting of waterlilies.

But we haven't been there since before Daddy's accident.

"Really?" I ask hopefully. "We can go there tomor-row?"

"Really," Mama replies.

"Weawy," Gabby echoes.

"Do you want to see the big flower painting tomor-row, Gabby girl?" I ask.

"Yes!" she says. "And see the pen-dwins!"

"The penguins?" Mama says blankly. And then we both realize what Gabby means.

She wants to go to the California Academy of Sci-ences, which is a mix of natural history museum and aquarium and planetarium. There's even a rain forest. And a colony of real African penguins.

It's one of our favorite places to go. But it's not free. We used to get a membership through the school when Mama was a teacher, but she's not a teacher anymore.

I'm in the midst of saying, "Probably not, Gabby girl," when Mama exclaims, "Yes!"

I gape at her.

"We're still members," she explains. "I com-pletely forgot until just now. Dr. Spalding renewed our membership. Just to be nice, because they know how much we love the Academy."

Mama pauses. "You know," she says, "we could even eat there. Remember, they have that quinoa bowl that Gabby can eat." She looks down at Gabby. "Great idea, Gabby girl."

"But, Mama," I say quietly, hoping Gabby won't pay attention. "I know we can get in for free, but how can we afford to eat there?"

We haven't eaten at any kind of restaurant in months.

"We get a discount in the café with our membership," Mama explains. "And we need to eat, right?"

"But, Mama—" I begin again.

She cuts me off. "Oh, my Maya. You've had so much to worry about. I'm sorry, love. We can do this tomorrow. I think we need to celebrate. And you"—she looks at me pointedly—"didn't eat anything for breakfast this morning."

"I just wanted Gabby to have enough," I say. "I didn't want her to be hungry and fussy while you were at your interview."

"Well," Mama says. "Thank you. I . . . thank you. But please don't do that again, okay? I'll find more food for Gabby when she needs it. We'll figure it out."

"Okay," I agree. And then I remember. "Mama! I have seventeen dollars and thirty-two cents. I thought I lost it, but I have it. It's in my backpack. We can use some of that to buy food! Please, Mama? Can we please use some of my money?"

She smiles. "Thanks, my Maya. You know what? Maybe you can use a little of that money to get yourself a treat tomorrow."

She looks at me intently for a second. "I have a feeling you could use a treat."

3:17 p.m. We're about half a block away from the bus stop when I notice a new Little Free Library in front of someone's house. It's shaped like a San Francisco Victorian house and painted pink with yellow trim.

"Can we stop, Mama?" I ask.

"Of course!" she says. She holds the umbrella over me as I hoist Gabby up, and we both peek inside.

I almost don't believe what I see.

Underneath the TAKE A BOOK; RETURN A BOOK sign, in the middle of a row of paperbacks, is a copy of *Charlie and the Chocolate Factory*. I put Gabby down and reach to pull it out. It's worn but intact. It's not the same version I had for so long, but the story will be the same. I show it to Mama.

"Your favorite book!" Mama says. "But that's one I know you have already," she says with a smile.

I shake my head. "Not anymore."

"What do you mean?" Mama asks.

"It was . . . I lost it today." I sigh. "I'll tell you the whole story soon, but not now, okay?"

"Okay," she says.

"May I take this one, even though I don't have a book to leave?" I ask.

"In this case," Mama says, "yes. Absolutely. I know you won't forget to leave a book when you can."

"I won't," I say, rubbing my thumb gently over the slightly raised letters of the title on the cover.

Gabby reaches for the book. "What's dis, my Maya?" she asks.

"It's *Charlie and the Chocolate Factory*," I say. "And we get to keep it, for now."

"Wead it!" Gabby says.

I laugh. "We will, before bed. But right now we have a bus to catch."

13

FAMiLY TiMe

Although the world is full of suffering,
it is full also of the overcoming of it.

—HELEN KELLER

3:49 p.m. We have to change buses once to get to the hospital where my dad is, but the second bus drops us off right in front. Which is a good thing, because the rain started pounding hard again while we were on the bus. Our huge umbrella can't keep us completely dry, even on the short walk to the entrance.

When we get inside, we're all shivering. An older man at the information desk recognizes us and smiles. "What a storm!" he exclaims. "Do you want to leave your umbrella here, hon?"

I don't want to leave it. We need it. Mama hesitates, too. "I'll keep an eye on it. Promise," he says very seriously, looking at me.

"Thanks, Ike," Mama says. She always remembers everyone's name.

3:52 p.m. We take the elevator to the eleventh floor, and Sabrina is waiting for us. She gives us quick hugs and then whispers, "Let's go in right now while Karen's on her break. And we're going to have to make it pretty quick. She's not going to like this."

3:54 p.m. Mama picks up Gabby and we all hurry behind Sabrina, who leads us to my dad's room. There's hand sanitizer outside the room, and we all use it before we go in. Inside it's dim and mostly quiet, except for some beeping. It takes a moment for my eyes to adjust after the bright lights of the hallways, but when they do, I can see him.

His face was pretty beat-up after the crash, but it's mostly healed. And now there's no huge tube going into his mouth, so I can really see him. His brown eyes aren't open, and he doesn't give me his goofy smile, but still.

He looks almost like himself again.

* * *

3:55 p.m. I stare at my dad and feel warmth in my chest. I imagine for a moment that it's morning and he's sleeping and I'm coming into his room to wake him up.

"Can I touch his hand?" I whisper to Sabrina.

"Of course, sweetie," she whispers back. "Just be gentle."

I walk over to my dad and softly put my hand on his. And I just stand there, watching him. I glance up at Mama and Gabby, and they're watching both of us. I see a tear slide down Mama's cheek. Then I look back at him.

To my surprise, at that moment his eyes flutter open. I don't know what he sees or if he knows me. But they're open. He's awake.

"I love you, Daddy," I whisper.

"Wuv you, Daddy," Gabby whispers from Mama's arms.

I'm probably imagining it, but I think maybe, just maybe, I see him smile. And it feels like the sun has just come out.

4:06 p.m. Sabrina has to rush us out of the room so we won't be there after visiting hours end. She keeps apologizing and telling us to come back tomorrow, which of course we will. I know that what she did for us could get her into trouble. I'm so happy my dad has her as one of his nurses. Mama hugs her. Gabby is in Mama's arms, and she pats Sabrina's cheek and says, "Thank you, Beena." Even Gabby can tell that Sabrina is looking out for us.

When we get back down to the lobby, we can see that the rain hasn't let up at all. Luckily, Ike has kept his promise and our umbrella is still there, behind his desk. He holds it in both hands and presents it to us as if it's a crown on a pillow or something, with a little bow and a smile.

"Oh, thank you, Ike," Mama says, and then glances out the window. "We're going to need it."

"It's waining, Mama!" Gabby says. She's right. In fact, it's raining harder than it has all day.

4:10 p.m. "You know," Mama says, glancing at her watch, "it's a little early, but let's go get something to eat here, now. Are you girls hungry?" she asks us.

"I hungwy, Mama!" Gabby says.

I'm hungry, too. After skipping breakfast and only getting one slice of pizza at lunch, thanks to Sloane, I feel like I'm starving, actually. But we've never paid for food here before. Mama tells me it's okay, that it's not too expensive. And I decide just to believe her.

In the checkout line I notice a jar of foil-wrapped

chocolate hearts. Mama notices them, too. "You can get one," she says quietly. "Just keep it on the down-low." That's what she always used to say if I wanted a treat that Gabby couldn't have. No need to rub it in.

"I'll buy it myself," I whisper.

"Oh, Maya . . ."

"Mama, I want to," I insist.

"Okay, love," she says. "Thank you."

So I hang back and choose a red heart, then pay for it with a little of my own money. I slip it into my sweatshirt pocket. I'm not sure when I'll eat it. Just looking forward to it is a pretty good treat, too.

5:13 p.m. We linger in the cafeteria after we finish eating, but then Mama notices that the rain has slowed down a bit. "We might want to go now," she says.

Gabby, feeling satisfied after her dinner, is getting very sleepy.

"Cawwy me!" she says, and Mama scoops her up.

I carry the umbrella.

When our bus pulls up at the stop in front of the hospital, the rain has slowed to a drizzle. So we hurry to the bus without putting the umbrella up, so Mama can keep holding Gabby.

Gabby's almost asleep when we get on the bus. We find two seats near the front. Gabby sits on Mama's lap and leans her head against Mama's shoulder. She dozes as the bus rattles along.

"Mama?" I say.

"Yes, love?" she asks, sounding a little drowsy.

"Could I . . ."

I stop. This feels hard. I was going to ask if I could sleep at Abby's house tomorrow night, but I change my mind.

"Could you what, my Maya?"

"Could I have a sleepover at Abby's house sometime? We haven't had one since . . . in a long time. And she keeps asking me and I keep saying no. She asked me for tomorrow night, but, Mama? I don't want to leave you and Gabby alone at the shelter."

Mama looks at me. "Maya, it's okay. You can have a sleepover tomorrow."

"I really don't want to," I say, realizing that it's true. "Not right now."

Even if it means sleeping at the shelter instead of sleeping in Abby's cozy extra bed, I need to stay with my family. We are each other's shelter.

"But, Maya—" Mama begins.

I cut her off. "I need to be with you and Gabby. And I think you need me, too."

She puts her free arm around me.

"I do need you, my Maya. I love you."

"I love you, too," I say.

I take a deep breath. I need to tell her something else. "Mama," I say, "I told Abby about the shelter today. I wanted to tell her the truth. Is that okay?"

"Of course it's okay," Mama says. "You can't keep all the hard things to yourself."

5:29 p.m. The rain is still coming down hard when it's time to change buses, but the bus shelter keeps us mostly dry. I hold the umbrella while Mama holds Gabby. Buses are slower in the rain, so we wait a long time for the next one.

At last the bus arrives, and we climb on. This one is crowded, and there are no seats. We're jostled and pushed as we find a place to stand and hang on, and Gabby wakes up.

"Sweep, Mama. I want to sweep!" Gabby begs, but there's no way she can sleep here. It's a slow, cramped, smelly journey. Gabby fusses for most of the way, until finally, finally, we reach our stop.

6:05 p.m. It takes a while to get through the crowd and off the bus, but eventually we do, just before the bus rolls away. We're back near our shelter.

And we're all glad to be here.

As we walk the blocks from the bus stop to the

shelter, we pass the tent camps that spring up along the sidewalks every evening, where dozens of homeless people spend the night. I look for the man in the orange sleeping bag, the one I saw this morning and was scared to walk by. I don't see him. I hope he's found a dry place where he can sleep inside tonight.

But I do see a little boy snuggled with his mother. My heart aches for him, and for all of them, knowing how cold and wet they're going to be tonight.

I wish we had something to give them. And then I remember the little chocolate heart in my pocket.

"Mama," I whisper. "Can I give that boy my chocolate heart?"

Mama looks surprised, but only for a second.

"But you . . . yes. Yes, you can," she says.

I reach into my pocket for the heart and carry it with my hand extended as I get closer to the little boy. I don't want to startle them, but he sees me and realizes I have something for him. I look at his mother to make sure it's okay. She looks confused at first but gives me a slight nod.

The boy and I don't speak to each other, but he smiles when he takes the heart.

I know it doesn't fix anything, but I'm glad I had something to share.

14

ReST TiMe

Where Thou art—that—is Home

—EMILY DICKINSON

6:25 p.m. An awning outside our shelter protects us from the rain as Mama shakes out our new umbrella and folds it up, then reaches into her backpack for a key. There's a lamp glowing on the front desk. When we get inside, it's warm and dry.

Angela, the woman who always works the Friday-night shift, looks up from her book and smiles at us. "Hi, ladies," she says. "Did you feel like you were swimming on the way here? I sure did."

Gabby laughs. "We did not swim!" she exclaims. "We walked!"

The rest of us laugh.

We pass the playroom and hear a volunteer finishing up story time for the kids staying in the shelter. Most are there with a parent, some of them are already in pajamas, and a few are standing close to the book, so they can look for the mouse in *Goodnight Moon.*

I see Haya there with her little brothers and sisters snuggled around her. They look peaceful. I give a little wave, and she waves back. Tomorrow morning I hope I'll see her for some art and chess before Mama, Gabby, and I leave for the day. And I find I'm not dreading a weekend at the shelter as much as I have before. Here, I don't have to worry about being made fun of or having my secret discovered. Here, everyone knows we're homeless—and also understands that we're much more than that. So are they.

Mama, Gabby, and I listen to the last few lines of the book: *Goodnight stars. Goodnight air. Goodnight noises everywhere.*

Then we head upstairs to our room.

6:39 p.m. We unlock our door and hang Mama's and Gabby's wet jackets and my wet sweatshirt on the hook on the back of the door. We take off our wet shoes and socks. We wash our hands, change into dry pajamas, and then brush our teeth. I'm wearing my hearts again, of course, but they're dry and familiar and they feel good. Mama gives me a dry pair of socks to sleep in, too. That means she won't have clean socks for tomorrow, but it means my feet will get all the way warm tonight.

"Thank you, Mama," I say.

She responds with a kiss on my forehead. "I couldn't get through this without you," she whispers. "Thank *you*."

The three of us snuggle on the cot while Mama reads from our new-to-us copy of *Charlie and the Chocolate Factory*. Gabby falls asleep against Mama about two pages in.

When Mama's voice trails away as she dozes off midsentence, I take the book from her hands and put it on the floor. I switch off the light, then climb down onto my mattress and pull my blanket up to my chin.

7:35 p.m. I close my eyes and listen. It's still raining, but it has slowed down, and the sun might come out tomorrow.

For the first time in months, we have hope.

We don't have a house, but we have a roof over our heads and a dry place to sleep.

I have my friends and my teachers.

We have books and art and libraries and a museum

with a warm rain forest and even buses and covered bus stops.

We have nurses and hospital volunteers.

I have a dad whose lungs are healing, and I have Mama and Gabby, right here.

For tonight, that's all the shelter I need.

A NOTE ABOUT CHILDREN AND HOMELESSNESS

At the end of *Shelter,* Maya is feeling hopeful that her family's homelessness will soon come to an end. But for too many homeless children, that hope has not yet arrived.

More than 2.5 million children in the United States experience homelessness each year, according to the National Center on Family Homelessness. That's about one in every thirty children. In 2020, the National Center for Homeless Education reported that about 1.5 million children attend school while homeless. Families make up approximately 30 percent of the overall homeless population, and about half of the population of homeless shelters. As of the 2019 San Francisco Homeless Point-in-Time Count Report, more than eight thousand homeless people were living in San Francisco.

Given the recent challenges facing families, including a global pandemic and unemployment, all of these numbers are likely rising, which is devastating for children. Children experiencing homelessness are at greater risk for serious emotional, behavioral, and health problems, as well as hunger and violence. They may struggle in school, and they and their parents may experience sharply increased stress because of the lack of stability in their lives.

We can all find ways to help. For example, you can encourage your family to contact a local homeless shelter to learn if there are opportunities to volunteer or to donate—and donations of any size are helpful. You could organize a fundraiser for a shelter, or a food drive for a local pantry. Maybe you have extra school or art supplies to donate. Perhaps you have outgrown pajamas or winter coats, or you have books that you've read and would like to share with another child. Shelters often welcome donations of certain gently used items, but please make sure to find out in advance what they do and don't accept. Many shelters also have special holiday programs through which you can help homeless families.

And always choose to be kind. You never know what difficulties someone is facing in her life, whether it's a bad day, or a tough family situation, or homelessness. A homeless child may look like you and share many of your interests—favorite books, games, school subjects, and activities. Always remember that anyone who is homeless is also much more than that.

ACKNOWLEDGMENTS

Enormous thanks to my editor, Tricia Lin, for caring about Maya and giving her the best home, and for thoughtful, insightful, and compassionate guidance during every step of this process. Thanks also to the rest of the team at Random House, including Caroline Abbey, Michelle Nagler, Mallory Loehr, Michelle Cunningham, Jen Valero, Janet Foley, Barbara Bakowski, Jonathan Morris, John Adamo, and Dominique Cimina. Endless gratitude, always, to my agent, Stacey Glick. Thanks for believing in me and making magic happen. Thanks to the amazing Dr. Danielle Cameron, a real-life superhero, for assistance with medical details—any inaccuracies are mine. Thanks to everyone who read drafts of this book, including Jack Adams, Kerri Bowen, and the moms and daughters of the Literary Masters Sixth-Grade Book Club. Most of all, thanks to my daughter Ellie, my first reader, my teacher, my inspiration, my heart. I love you so much.

ABOUT THE AUTHOR

CHRISTIE MATHESON is the author and illustrator of several picture books, including *Tap the Magic Tree, Touch the Brightest Star,* and *Bird Watch.* This is her first novel. She lives in San Francisco with her family.

◎ @christiematheson